Philippa Fisher
and the
Dream-Maker's
Daughter

Philippa Fisher and the Dream-Maker's Daughter

LIZ KESSLER

illustrated by KATIE MAY

CANDLEWICK PRESS

Text copyright © 2009 by Liz Kessler
Illustrations copyright © 2009 by Katie May

First U.S. paperback edition 2010

Library of Congress Cataloging-in-Publication Data is available.

Library of Congress Catalog Card Number 2008938410

ISBN 978-0-7636-4202-0 (hardcover)
ISBN 978-0-7636-4829-9 (paperback)

12 13 14 15 16 17 RRC 12 11 10 9 8 7 6 5 4

Printed in Crawfordsville, IN, U.S.A.

This book was typeset in Hightower and Maiandra.

Candlewick Press
99 Dover Street
Somerville, Massachusetts 02144

visit us at www.candlewick.com

For Laura
Because you helped so much more
than you realize, and because you love
Philippa and Daisy as much as I do

Contents

The deeper that sorrow carves into your being,
the more joy you can contain.

— KAHLIL GIBRAN
FROM *THE PROPHET*

ATC

"We have a problem."

"What is it?"

"We're nearly out of time. There's only a matter of weeks left."

"So what's the problem?"

"The child. We all know the conditions that were set."

"Yes, and?"

"And she hasn't met them yet. Her heart is closed."

"Give me the file."

"Here it is. It's all up to date, just—"

"She needs a friend."

"Someone to talk to . . ."

". . . Open up to."

"Exactly."

"Can't you check the files? There must be something in there that can help."

"Done. I've cross-referenced everything—twice. I couldn't find anything."

"Nothing at all?"

"Well, there's just one possibility. It's an outside chance, but there was a case earlier this year. The friendship score was the highest ever."

"Show me."

"Here it is. I've already located that client. She might be just what we need—if only we could get her in the right place."

"So, how do you propose we do that?"

"We could use the fairy from the original assignment. I know we wouldn't normally match a fairy godmother with the same client twice, but that girl may be our best chance. We just need to get her here, set up a few meetings—"

"Do it! Get that fairy godmother on the case, and let's get moving. We haven't got a moment to lose."

chapter one
DECISION

So here's the situation. You've won tickets for your whole family to take a vacation anywhere you like. What do you do?

Most normal people would start with the Internet, or a brochure or two, perhaps a travel agent. My parents? Thirteen different road maps, two atlases, and a box of pushpins. That's what you need to plan a vacation in *our* house. And this was day three of planning. Remember, I said *normal* people do it the other way — the easy way.

I grabbed a magazine and left them to it.

*   *   *

"How about the Poconos?" Dad asked, opening up the fourth map and laying it on top of the others across the kitchen table. "We've never been there."

"Yes, we have. Don't you remember? We were on our way to visit friends and ran out of gas, so we had to stay there for the night."

"Oh, yes. A little hilly, wasn't it?"

Mom leaned farther across the map, knocking a cup of cold coffee all over the mountain range — and herself. "What about Florida?" she asked, wiping her shirt with a tea towel.

"Too far."

"New York?"

"Too near."

I got up from my stool and joined them at the table. "Mom. Dad. You know, this is . . ."

Dad looked up as my voice trailed off. Mom was too busy opening the box of pushpins to notice the hesitation in my voice. "Come on, let's just stick one of these in a place and go for it," she said. She was on a mission. She started rolling up the tea towel that she'd just used to mop up the coffee. "We'll do it blindfolded," she announced firmly.

"'This is' what?" Dad asked, stopping to look at me. "What is it, sweetheart?"

This is supposed to be my *vacation*, I wanted to say. *This is my prize.*

I'd won it at the school's talent show at the end of the year. Tickets for my parents and me to go anywhere we liked. Anywhere *I* liked. I was the one who'd won them! We'd been planning to go in the summer, but my parents had had lots of parties booked. Their party-entertaining business is at its busiest in the summer, so we'd ended up having to postpone the trip to my fall-break vacation.

I looked into Dad's eyes. They were dark and tired. He smiled his goofy smile at me, and I couldn't help softening. He deserved a vacation as much as I did. So did Mom. They'd both worked really hard all summer without a real break at all. At least I'd had a week away at Charlotte's — if you could count that.

I took Dad's hand in mine. "This is fun," I said, forcing a smile. "Go on — I'll go first."

Mom stood behind me and tied the tea towel around my head. "No peeping, now," she said. "Just stick the pin in the map, and wherever it lands, that's where we'll go!"

"Unless it's in the middle of a city," Dad said.

"Or in the middle of the ocean," Mom added.

"Or a building site," I chipped in, finally letting their puppy-dog enthusiasm infect me. I reached into the box of pushpins and took one out. I was about to stick it into the map when Dad grabbed my arm. "Wait!" he yelled.

"What?"

"Look!" he said, ignoring the fact that I had a coffee-stained tea towel wrapped over my eyes. I pulled the towel off and rubbed my face.

I saw it right away. A butterfly, fluttering over the map. It must have flown in through the window.

"It's beautiful," Mom said.

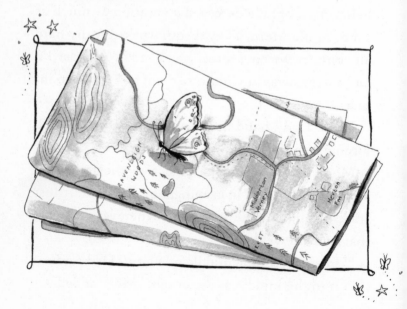

"I've never seen markings like that before," Dad added, silently bending over the table. "So intricate."

"So pretty," I said, watching as it flew the length of the map, twisting this way and that, in tight little circles and figure eights. Its wings buzzing and vibrating, it hovered just above the map, as though searching for the perfect place to land.

It finally chose a spot in the top corner of the map, and we all leaned in to take a closer look.

"Careful," Mom whispered. "Don't want to frighten it away."

The butterfly maneuvered slowly across the map, wings open, like an airplane taxiing to the runway. Its wings were so delicate. They looked as though they'd been made from the thinnest silk in the world and decorated with the tiniest brushes that could possibly exist. Dark purple lines wriggled all around the tips, which were dotted with baby pink spots. Dark purple faded to ocean blue at the center of each wing.

"Amazing," I said.

"Nature's incredible, isn't it?" Dad murmured.

"Hang on a sec." Mom tilted her head to peer under the butterfly on the map. "Look at that," she said.

"We are looking at it," Dad said with a laugh. "Can't you see us? This is us looking at it."

"Not at the butterfly!" Mom said, pointing at the map. "At where it's landed."

The map showed a patch of green bushes and stick pictures of trees, with a straggly blue line weaving in between them.

"A forest with a river running through it," Dad said. "What about it?"

"It's exactly what we're looking for!" Mom said.

"It's certainly not in the middle of a city," I said.

"Or in the middle of the ocean," Dad added, winking at me.

"Or a building site!" Mom concluded.

"Ravenleigh Woods," I read from just below the butterfly's wings. "Sounds nice."

"Doesn't it?" Mom said dreamily. "Kind of romantic."

"That's where we're going, then?" Dad asked.

Mom and I looked at each other. The butterfly fluttered its wings. "Yes!" I said.

"Why not?" Mom agreed. "A butterfly's as good as a pushpin."

Which is quite a strange thing to say, if you think

about it, but I rarely question the way my parents' minds work. At this point I was just happy a decision had been made. Anything that meant we could get rid of the maps that were beginning to take over the house.

"Good. I agree. I'll start checking out local B&Bs," Dad said. He squeezed my hand before pulling Mom over toward him. Twirling her in a circle, he danced her across the kitchen floor. Mom's skirt flowed around her as Dad spun her. While they giggled and whirled around the kitchen, I started putting away the maps.

The butterfly was still sitting in the same spot. I stopped and looked at it again. It turned to face me, its tiny, goggly bug eyes trained on mine.

"Hey, I know you're only a butterfly and all that, but you just did me a big favor," I said. "It's taken us three days to make that decision!"

And you know what? A moment later, I swear the butterfly replied. I mean, I know that it didn't really give an *actual* reply — obviously. It was probably the wind blowing through the window, ruffling the maps. But it sounded like words. And it sounded as though it came from the butterfly.

See you there.

I glanced over my shoulder to see if Mom and Dad had heard it, but they were too busy jiving around the kitchen to notice anything else. It was just the wind. I laughed at myself. I was at it again.

You see, an incredible thing happened to me a little while ago. I had a fairy of my very own! Honestly, it's true. Well, she wasn't actually *mine*. Daisy always made sure to point out that she didn't *belong* to me — but she was on an assignment that involved giving me three wishes. By the time she'd finished, it had become more than an assignment. We became like real friends — best friends, even.

That was months ago now, and it seemed I still couldn't stop hoping to find magic everywhere. To be honest, it was more that I wanted Daisy to come back. I looked for evidence of fairies and magic in everything. I was even trying to convince myself that a butterfly had talked to me now! I laughed out loud as I looked back at the map.

But, just for fun, I whispered back, "Yeah, see you there."

The second I'd spoken, the butterfly slowly opened and closed its wings, as if it were clapping. Then it inched up off the map, rising like a helicopter. It was almost as though it had waited for me to reply before leaving.

A moment later, it flew straight out the window — and was gone.

I shook my head, laughing quietly at myself. Then I folded up the map and thought nothing more of it.

I waited on the highest branch of the farthest tree in the forest, as I'd been told. The view was incredible from up here. The tops of the trees waved in the breeze, their leaves rustling softly, as though they were whispering to the rest of the forest to be quiet.

Shhhhhhhhhhh.

A patch of sunlight flickered in between the leaves, growing into a sparkling fan on the forest's floor. Tiny triangular rainbows danced in its light.

My supervisor had arrived.

"Good work, Daisy. You did well."

"Is she coming?"

"They'll be here next week."

Next week! I was really going to see Philippa again, after all this time! "I will be able to meet up with her, won't I?" I asked.

"Daisy, we can't make any promises. Your special mission was to bring her here. You've done that, and we're grateful. But you still have your own job to get on with at Triple D."

"A job where she'll be right on the doorstep!"

"Even so. We can't allow any distractions from our main objective."

"Which is what?" I asked briskly. I knew better than to talk to FGSunray239 disrespectfully, but I couldn't stop myself. Spikes of annoyance were growing inside me so sharply they were making my wings itch.

The sunlight faded slightly. "I'm afraid I can't tell you that."

"Why not? If it concerns Philippa, it concerns me. She's my friend." *My best friend*, I added under my breath.

"Daisy, in your previous assignment with this client, you showed a high level of personal involvement."

"So? I completed the job, didn't I?"

"You did indeed—and you did it very well." FGSunray239 smiled, and the treetops sparkled for a moment, as if grateful for her warmth. "Your compassion for the child was fully in keeping with your assignment. But too much personal attachment can be dangerous, and in your case it made you careless."

"Careless? What do you mean?"

"I'm referring to your ability to keep confidential information to yourself. For this reason, your role in this part of the assignment is now over."

"I won't do it again," I said feebly—although in my heart I wasn't so sure. I wanted to share *everything* with Philippa! That was what you did with a best friend, wasn't it?

"Maybe you wouldn't," FGSunray239 said. "But we can't take any risks. A high degree of confidentiality is needed for this mission, or it will fail. And Daisy . . ."

"What?" I looked up, dazzled by the light shining brightly before me.

"A high-ranking fairy godmother is watching this case very closely and has let us know, in no uncertain terms, that we must *not* allow this mission to fail."

Despite the warmth of the sunlight all around, I felt a shiver sneak through me, making my wings flutter and twitch. "I understand," I said.

"Good. Now put this extra task out of your mind and

go back to your job. You have work to do. There's a new delivery waiting for you."

And with that, FGSunray239 disappeared, taking the sparkling light with her and leaving the trees to continue whispering among themselves.

Well, this is nice, isn't it?" Mom called from the living room as Dad and I lugged our bags into the kitchen.

We'd decided to rent a cottage in the end. We'd managed to track down a couple of B&Bs in the area, but they were full. There was a big swanky hotel about five miles down the road, with two swimming pools and a Jacuzzi and entertainment every night, but Mom and Dad didn't want that. "Not our scene," they said.

I would have argued—swimming every day for

a week in a heated pool; how could that not be any-one's scene? — till I saw the hotel's dress code. The brochure said guests had to be "neatly attired at all times." At mealtimes, ties for the men and eve-ning dresses for women were "encouraged." The thought of my parents dressed up in evening wear was the biggest laugh I'd had all year. They didn't often stray from their jeans and tie-dyed T-shirts with Greenpeace slogans on them.

And the idea of having to accompany them seven nights in a row while they tried to behave like nor-mal grown-ups was a stress that even two swimming pools and a Jacuzzi couldn't outweigh. No, the rented cottage would be just fine. The compromise was that they'd said we'd see if we could get guest passes and go swimming for a day while we were here.

A fence ran around the cottage, beyond which tall, thin trees stretched almost higher than I could see, their branches reaching out toward the roof and tickling the upstairs windows. There was a gate behind the cottage that led directly into the forest.

"It's all right here," Dad said, opening every door he could find and sticking his nose in every cup-board. There were two patio doors leading from the

kitchen out to a small garden. A few rays of late-afternoon sun beamed in, lighting up a small patch on the floor.

I joined Mom in the living room. A fireplace was filled with logs, and a comfy sofa and two big cozy-looking chairs stood facing it, all ready to be snuggled into. Behind them, shelves were stacked from floor to ceiling with books and games.

"Scrabble," Mom said. "Great! But I bet half the letters are missing."

I headed upstairs to check out the bedrooms.

The floorboards creaked and groaned as I

inspected each room. At the end of the corridor, there was a big double bedroom with a four-poster bed and a connected bathroom. That would be Mom and Dad's room, no doubt. At the other end of the corridor, the floor sloped past another bathroom and down to a second bedroom. It had a four-poster bed, too, with curtains draped all around it. Yikes — a bit too much for me!

I was turning to go back downstairs when I noticed another staircase in the hall. It was more like a ladder, with chunky wooden steps leading almost vertically up to a trapdoor. It sort of reminded me of our tree house at home.

I climbed the stairs and stuck my head through the trapdoor. Another bedroom. Smaller than the other two, it had just a single bed with a tiny table next to it. A long wooden beam stretched across the ceiling. A square window with a big metal frame sat in the middle of a low stone wall on one side. The front half of the ceiling sloped down all the way to the floor. I hitched myself up into the room. There was only just enough room to stand! It was like a secret den.

I wondered who used to live in this room. It must

have been a child. A grown-up would have been too tall. Maybe it was a girl like me. Someone I could have been friends with. I would have enjoyed coming over to visit and hanging out with her up here.

When we'd booked the cottage, the owners had said we were almost the first to rent it. The family who used to live here had only sold it to them in the last year. I couldn't help wondering where the family had gone to and why they would sell such a lovely house.

Either way, this was definitely going to be my room!

I ran downstairs to get my bags. Mom was still exploring the living room. "They've got lots of games," she said vaguely as I got my bags from the kitchen and dragged them past her.

Dad had found some leaflets and spread them out on the table in the middle of the living room. "Lots going on around here," he said, flicking through the leaflets. "Hey, there's salsa dancing on Tuesdays."

I prepared myself for a week of being embarrassed by my parents. Which was quite easy to do. My parents embarrassed me most of the time, so I was pretty much always prepared.

"There's a stone circle near here, too," Dad murmured.

"Ooh, is there a full moon this week?" Mom replied, coming into the kitchen and joining him at the table. I tried not to despair as I headed back upstairs with my bags.

I lay on the bed, looking around my bedroom. It was like a sanctuary, my own little hiding place from the world. The only thing wrong with it was — well, it would have been nice to share it. I felt a little bubble of sadness rise inside me. If this had been like our old vacations, Charlotte would probably have been with me.

Charlotte's my best friend. Or *was* my best friend. It was still really hard to admit that we'd grown apart. She and her family moved away last year, and our lives had quickly started going in different directions. We kept in touch for a while with e-mails and an occasional phone call. I even went to stay with her in the summer, but it was a disaster. It was so strange; despite knowing each other nearly all our lives, we found we didn't have anything to say to each other after the first couple of days. I spent most of the week wanting to go home. Things hadn't been the same between us since I'd met Daisy.

Charlotte is one of those types who thinks reality is reality. Which, when you put it like that, is quite hard to argue with, I suppose. But I think there's more to life than just the things that make sense!

When it was simply a case of our having different opinions, it wasn't so important. I didn't mind Charlotte laughing at my theories about how rays of sun poking through a cloud might be channels for carrying messages from another dimension. I kind of laughed at it myself, and it was part of the fun we shared.

But it all changed with Daisy. Daisy really *was* a fairy! A fairy godmother! Or fairy godsister; that was what we decided she'd be called. It made more sense, seeing as she was the same age as me. But the point is — she was real. And no amount of logical argument could convince me that she wasn't. I *saw* her, *talked* to her, made *friends* with her. And she changed my life when she gave me three wishes — even if the biggest change was that I discovered my life was pretty good as it was.

Once I knew that fairies existed for real, I wasn't OK with Charlotte laughing at me anymore. I tried telling her about Daisy in a letter. I'd hoped that maybe this one time, she'd believe me, that she'd see I was telling her something that really mattered to me. So when her response was to give me the usual stream of facts and figures explaining why fairies were a physical impossibility, well, I guess something changed for me after that.

From then on, I stopped wanting to share things with Charlotte so much. What was the point? For one thing, she was living hundreds of miles away, and from the sound of her e-mails, she was getting more and more involved in her new life and further away from the one we used to share. And for another, why bother trying to explain things to someone who tells you that the things you really believe in are a bunch of jokes and nonsense?

I actually did ask her if she wanted to come on vacation with us. Part of me wanted her to, hoping that perhaps we'd get our old friendship back if we spent some time together, away from all her new things — just the two of us with my parents. But a bigger part of me was nervous that if she did, we'd end up spending another week having nothing to say to each other. So when she said that she couldn't leave her pony and her new puppy, I was honestly more relieved than disappointed. It felt horrible to admit it, but it was true.

It didn't stop me from feeling a bit lonely now; although when I thought about the week ahead, it was Daisy I wished I could be sharing it with, not Charlotte.

But Daisy was even more out of my life than Charlotte. She'd done her assignment, and that was that. No matter how much I wished I could see her again, or looked for scraps of evidence that she was still around, it was probably time I faced that truth as well. Daisy was gone, and she wasn't coming back. Charlotte and I had grown apart. And I still hadn't found a new best friend at school. Which meant that right now, things weren't going so well, actually.

I slowly unpacked my clothes, putting them away in the tiny chest of drawers under the window.

"Philippa!" Mom called from landing. "We're going out to explore the village. You coming?"

"Two minutes," I called down. I threw the rest of my clothes on the bed and joined them downstairs.

Mom was unwrapping a dish she'd brought from home and putting it in the oven. "Lentil bake," she said. "Should be ready in half an hour."

"Right; let's hit the town!" Dad said with a grin. Then, looping my arm in his, he made me copy his silly walk all the way into the village.

Well, I always had Mom and Dad, I reminded myself. They might be the ditziest dingbats on the planet, but at least they hadn't deserted me.

Hitting the town didn't take long.

There were three main roads that led into the center of the village, where a group of shops and a couple of restaurants huddled around a cobbled square. A secondhand bookshop, three gift shops, a grocery store, and a deli. They were mostly closed, so we had to settle for window shopping.

Mom spotted some clay dragons in the window of one of the gift shops; it was called Potluck. "Oh, look at these!" she enthused. "We have to come back and get one of them."

Dad peered through the glass, his head cocked almost upside down. "Not at that price, we don't!" he sputtered. "Nearly two hundred dollars for that one!"

I scanned the shopwindow. As well as the dragons — which took up half the window — there were brightly painted cups and saucers, enormous plates with writing all around the edges, photo frames with prints of baby-size feet in blues and pinks all over them, plant pots, piggy banks, all huddled together on the wide shelves.

"Oh, look," Mom said. She was pointing to a poster in the middle of the window.

"'Make a mug. Paint a plate. Pottery sessions for the whole family,'" I read.

"That sounds like fun, don't you think?" Mom squealed excitedly. "We could make things for each other."

"Good idea. At two hundred dollars apiece, it's about time one of us became a professional dragon-maker!" Dad said with a wink. Then he looked more closely. "Hey, that's the same as one of the leaflets in the cottage," he said. "Said something about a special offer this week: half price or something."

"What d'you think? Shall we check it out one day?" Mom asked, looking at me.

At least it would keep me busy; it might even

stop me from feeling so miserable and lonely. "Why not?" I said.

"Right. That's settled," Dad said. Then, grabbing my arm and looping it back over his, he silly-walked me back to the cottage.

"Almost dinnertime!" he announced. "There's a slice of lentil bake in that kitchen with my name on it."

Which, knowing the bizarreness of my mom's dishes, there probably was.

Mom poked her head through the trapdoor. "You sure you'll be OK up here, sweetheart?" she asked.

"Of course I will," I replied over the top of the blankets. I loved my little den, even if the bed did sag like a deep well in the middle, and the blankets itched a bit and felt tight all around the edges where they were tucked in. It was still cozy.

"As long as you're sure," Mom said, hitching herself up the steps and crawling over to the side of my bed. "Night-night, darling," she said, kissing my forehead. "Sleep well. Sweet dreams."

"You, too," I replied. Once she'd gone, I switched off my light and shut my eyes, suddenly tired out.

Maybe it was from spending all day putting on a happy face for my parents. I didn't want to do anything to spoil their vacation. And anyway, I guess I was glad to be away from home as well. I just wished I had someone to share the trip with.

I turned over, pulling the covers with me, but I couldn't get comfortable. Moments later, I threw them off again, restless and indecisive.

The blankets made my arms itch, and my back was starting to ache from the dip in the mattress. I shifted to the edge of the bed and turned over again.

It was no use. I couldn't sleep. How long had I been lying here? As I tossed and turned, I grew more and more irritable. Desperate for sleep, I tried counting sheep, counting clouds, counting stars — but nothing worked.

I pushed the blankets to the bottom of the bed. It was a hot night. Why was it so hot? Why couldn't I sleep when I was so tired?

My mind raced and scrambled, until eventually I drifted off into a jerky, dreamless sleep.

Tap, tap, tap.

What was that? Something had woken me. I lifted my head off the pillow and listened. Nothing. I let my head drop back down on the pillow again and was on the verge of falling back to sleep, when—

Tappity-tap, tap, tap.

What was it? Something at the window? My head was heavy and full of sleep.

I peered into the darkness of my bedroom. Nothing. It was probably just one of those huge trees that stretched higher than the roof, its branches hitting the windowpane, scratching at the glass.

I pressed the pillow over my ear and tried to settle back to sleep. But the tapping carried on, growing louder and more insistent.

Tap, tap, taptaptaptap, TAP!

Eventually, I dragged myself out of bed. Kneeling down at the window, I lifted the latch and pushed the window frame. Nothing happened. I pushed harder, but the window was jammed. I pushed again and again, bashing at the frame with my fist. Nothing. Frustration grew inside me, coiling up like a tight spring in my chest.

Come on, open! What's wrong with you?

I peered at the frame through the glow from the bedside lamp. It had been painted down. Surely paint couldn't be that strong? *One more try.*

I hit the frame as hard as I could with the palm of my hand. Finally the window creaked and the paint cracked. I bashed again, nudging it open, bit by bit, but then my hand slipped and I hit the glass, too. It splintered all along the edge and I froze, silently watching to see if the glass was going to shatter and fall out of its frame.

A tiny sliver had split from the side, but apart from that, it was still in one piece. There was a crack running along the edge of the glass, but you could hardly see it. I decided not to worry about it. One tiny piece of glass missing from the edge of the frame wasn't going to hurt anyone!

I opened the window, and the night air rushed in to meet me, fanning my face and soothing my rattled mind.

I leaned out of the window, sticking my face right out and taking a few deep breaths. It felt as if I were breathing the whole forest into me, and I shivered as its cool stillness seeped into the room.

A tiny crescent moon hung low in the sky, as though dangling from an invisible string, like a hammock, lazy and peaceful. The night was completely still.

That was when I realized—there were no branches near my bedroom. Nothing in scratching distance of the window at all. Had I imagined the tapping? I couldn't have—it had woken me up!

But there was nothing here.

Something caught my eye, glinting against the blackness. It was flickering in the ivy below the window, catching the tiny bit of light from the moon.

It glinted again, just out of reach, not near enough to have caused the tapping. Then I saw what it was. The glass—the splinter that had broken from the window—it was stuck in something. I reached down toward it. My hand touched something smooth and feathery. Yikes! I yanked my hand back.

But I was intrigued. What *was* it? I reached out again and unhooked the whatever-it-was as carefully as I could. Bringing it inside, I sat down on the bed and examined it. A metal hoop, with feathers looped all around the edges. The circle was filled with tiny pieces of material all carefully sewn and woven together. The material was so delicate and thin, like a see-through skin of the smallest animal in the world. I'd never seen anything like it. Right in the center of the delicate skin, the shard of glass had pierced it and was lodged, like an archer's arrow on a bull's-eye.

I got up and shut the window. Then I hooked the feathery thing onto a jagged piece of wood sticking out of the beam above my bed.

Lying down again, I stared up at it, thinking that it reminded me of one of those mobiles you hang above babies' cradles and wishing it had a little wind-up machine inside so that it would turn around and around and play "Rock-a-Bye Baby." The thought made me smile. Or perhaps it was some kind of feathery lucky charm, like a symbol that ancient tribes used to worship. A feathered charm — yes, I liked that idea!

I was finally getting sleepy. Yawning, I told myself something that Dad used to say to me when I was little: if I made sure I still had a smile on my face as I fell asleep, I'd be certain to have happy dreams.

But then, what did Dad know?

Another minute and she'd have woken up—I'm sure she would have. Then I could have seen her.

I couldn't risk waiting, though. I'd sneaked out when I had a spare five minutes. I knew it wasn't long enough— and I knew I'd been warned not to. But still. What did they expect me to do? Sit around doing nothing while my best friend in the world was just down the road?

Well, they could think again. I just had to think of a way to sneak back tomorrow night.

But how? For a moment, I hesitated. Was I crazy? I knew ATC would be watching me closely on this assignment. I had to prove they could trust me, and I didn't want to blow it.

But on the other wing, I had Philippa right here, literally on my doorstep!

No. I couldn't ignore her. I wasn't going to waste another day. I *had* to see her.

I'd think of something. I'd find a way.

chapter three
POTLUCK

I can't see anything. Why can't I see anything?

It's so dark — too dark. It's pitch, pitch-black. More than that, even. It's like a complete absence of light, absence of everything. There's nothing. So much nothing that I want to cry.

I try to make my way through the emptiness. I'm on my knees, crawling, reaching out with my arms for something — anything. I feel like a blind man without his cane, hoping someone will notice him, flailing around, calling out.

Then I'm slipping through nothingness.

My hands hit something. A wall. I feel my way around it, inching up with my fingers. I pull myself out of the vacuum and stand in the darkness. Another wall on my other side. It's too near, closing in on me. A corridor. I walk forward — it's all I can do.

And then I see it. A bright light, ahead of me. I want to cry again, this time with happiness. The light — it's full of everything I want. There's a face inside it, looking at me, calling to me. A woman — what's she saying? I need to know what she's saying to me!

I'm running blindly down the corridor, running toward the light, toward the face. Wait!

But she's gone. Only the light remains. It keeps moving, changing, growing strong, then faint, disappearing altogether and then returning, strong and focused, almost blinding me.

"Philippa."

I have to get to the light. Don't go — don't go — stay!

"Philippa! What's wrong? You're shaking."

No, don't stop me! I have to get to the light. It's fading — disappearing. I can hardly see it now. Please! Come back!

"Philippa, you have to wake *up*!"

Mom was holding my shoulders. *What happened? Where's the light?*

"Darling, are you all right?"

I stared blankly at her.

"You were calling out."

I looked around the room, trying to take in the reality of it. Of course. It was just a dream. A nightmare. Nothing to worry about.

I took Mom's hand. "Sorry," I said.

Mom hugged me. "It's all right, sweetheart. I was still awake. I can never get to sleep the first night somewhere new. Shall I fix us a couple of hot chocolates?"

I sat up and pulled the blankets off me. "That would be great."

"You stay here," Mom said, tucking me back in. "I'll bring it up."

Mom left the room, and I snuggled down again, still unsettled by my dream. I could hardly remember what it had been about now; just the feeling remained — a huge feeling of sadness. I'd never felt this sad in my life. It was as if the sadness were bigger than me, as if it could swallow me up and I'd disappear completely.

I must have drifted back to sleep, because I don't remember Mom coming back. I woke in the morning with a dull ache inside me that I couldn't explain.

Reaching across to the bedside table, I gulped down the chocolate drink Mom had left me. Cold and bitter. My parents don't believe in normal hot chocolate, that is, hot chocolate that tastes like chocolate. It has to be free-trade, recycled, organic, and preferably stripped of flavor before it's allowed in our house. Still, my mouth was dry so I drank it down, only wincing a bit.

As I got dressed, I pushed the nightmare to the back of my mind, shaking off the strange sadness like a tree shaking off dead leaves.

*　　*　　*

The house was so quiet I could almost have believed my parents had gone out and left me there on my own. Except I knew them well enough to know that there wasn't a huge probability of their waking up before lunchtime if they didn't have to — and it was only ten-thirty.

I crept past their room, listening for any signs of life. Gentle snores came from the other side of the door. They were *so* predictable!

I went down to the kitchen and looked out at the garden. It was pouring rain outside. I guess that's what happens when you take your summer vacation in October.

"Morning, darling." Mom appeared behind me, her nightgown wrapped around her, her hair sticking out at every angle imaginable. "Thought I heard you."

"What are you doing up? Isn't this like the middle of the night for you and Dad?"

Mom ruffled my hair as she passed me, heading straight for the coffeemaker. "Ha, ha! Couldn't sleep. I told you — never can, somewhere new. I'm usually all right after the first night. I'll probably sleep like a log for the rest of the week. At least you got back to sleep after your bad dream. You were passed out when I came back up."

She opened the fridge, getting out the milk and reaching into the cupboard for the biggest mug she could find—which wasn't very big. "What do you want to do today, chicken? Go for a nice walk? We should get out and make the most of the country-side while we're here."

I nudged a thumb toward the French windows. "You have seen the weather, haven't you?"

Mom sat down beside me and looked out. "Oh," she said.

We sat in silence, listening to the coffeemaker grind into action.

"Hey, I know," Mom said, poking me with her elbow. "Let's go to one of those sessions at the pottery shop." She looked in disgust at her mug. "We could do with some decent-sized mugs!"

I'd rather have gone swimming. I was about to say so when Mom said, "Come on—it'll be fun," and looked at me with big, pleading eyes that made me wonder—as I often did—which of us was the parent and which was the child.

It was just as well I *wasn't* the parent. The pair of them would be spoiled brats. I could never say no to them. To be honest, I liked making them happy. Was that so wrong?

"OK," I said, smiling. "That's a great idea."

We could always go swimming another day.

"So, you can help yourself to any of these books. Have a look through to get ideas for pots. You can even copy straight from the picture, if there's one you particularly like."

The woman had short red hair tucked under a headband with multicolored flowers on it and bright green eyes that sparkled when she smiled — which she did a lot. She told us her name was Annie, and she showed us around the shop, pointing out little bits and pieces while she talked. Strange things that people had made, different casts we could use, paint trays with every color you could think of.

Everything was ordered and labeled, even the different types of coffee on a shelf at the back — and there were a lot of those as well! Mom was in heaven — especially when Annie said we could help ourselves whenever we wanted a refill.

"If you don't see the color of paint you want, just

let me know, and I'll mix it for you," Annie went on. "I'm here to help — so don't sit there wondering what to do. Just be creative and have fun!"

Something about her manner had already cheered me up. She seemed to radiate a happy feeling. The shop made you feel like you were being wrapped up in a blanket and put in front of a fire with a hot chocolate. Or maybe it was just the fact that the heat was on and it was still pouring outside. Either way, I realized I was glad we'd come.

Annie showed us to a table. "This is where you can work. Just let me know if you have any questions, OK?" She caught my eye, and a tiny shiver ran through me. Her eyes were so sharp — I had the feeling that they could see all the way inside my mind, that she could read my thoughts. Then she smiled her warm smile again, and I realized I was being silly. My imagination really was working overtime today!

"I just need to make a quick phone call," Annie said. She headed for the back of the shop and picked up the phone.

A moment later, I could hear snatches of her conversation.

"... *So* glad it was you who picked up the

phone . . . could do with some help . . . will he let you, d'you think? . . . OK, great. See you soon. . . ."

I wandered over to the books of pictures, trying not to eavesdrop. Annie had finished her conversation now anyway, and was busy tidying the paint pots into neat rows.

I glanced at the other tables on my way past. There was a young couple at one of them, sitting opposite each other and painting a huge plate together. They hadn't looked up since we'd been in here. Too busy giggling and squealing and reaching across the table to hold hands. A family of four was working quietly at another table: the parents hunched over their bowls, a young boy frowning seriously, his tongue poking out of his mouth as he drew around his hand onto a mug, and a toddler splattering paint onto a plate.

Mom and Dad had decided to launch in without looking at any of the books. No doubt they'd come up with the most flamboyant paintings for their mugs. Mine would look really boring compared with whatever they did. Not that I minded. I was used to it. Mom and Dad rarely did anything you couldn't notice from a mile away.

I'd just settled down to flip through a book of

pictures when the doorbell tinkled and a girl came in. She had deep brown eyes and long blond hair that fell over one shoulder. She was wearing denim shorts and woolly tights and a fluffy sweater with a couple of silver dog tags around her neck. She looked like the kind of girl who wouldn't notice me in a million years. Far too cool and pretty and trendy for the likes of me.

She stood in the doorway, fiddling with the hem of her shorts as she looked around the shop.

"Robyn!" Annie went running over to the door and threw her arms around the girl.

"Annie." Robyn relaxed into the hug.

I watched them out of the corner of my eye, my head still in the book I was holding. I didn't want to look nosy.

Robyn pulled away. "I thought you said you were busy," she said. "There's hardly anyone here!"

Annie stroked Robyn's hair. "I know. I just wanted to see you," she said with a quick smile. "Was your father OK about you coming over?"

Robyn shrugged as she fiddled with the dog tags around her neck. "I said I was going for a walk."

Annie lowered her voice. I could still hear her,

though. Everyone else had gone quiet except the toddler, who was happily chatting away to himself. "He doesn't know you're here? Robyn—"

"He's fine." Robyn waved Annie's concern away with a flick of her hand. "Probably glad to get rid of me," she added with what sounded to me like a false laugh. "I think he's already sick of me being around so much—and fall break has only just begun."

"What d'you mean?"

"I was trying to help him get a new system going in the shop. You know what it's like in there nowadays."

"No, not really. I haven't been in there for the last year," Annie said tightly. "You know that."

"Well, anyway, I only wanted to help, but he said I was getting in the way. He told me to get out from under his feet. So I'm sure he won't even miss me."

Annie's face turned even more serious. "I don't want to get you into trouble."

"Honestly, it's fine. He doesn't know I'm here, and there's no reason why he'll find out."

Annie thought for a moment. "Just this once, then," she said. "You know I prefer him to know when you meet up with me, even if he doesn't like

45

it." Then the warmth crept back into her eyes as she took Robyn's hand and led her to the counter at the back of the shop. "Come on, then. Let's fetch you an apron, and you can get started." She pointed to the table where Mom and Dad were sitting. "We've got a new family in today. Maybe you could help them. This is Mr. and Mrs. Fisher, and this is their daughter, Philippa."

I looked up from the book. "Hi," I said with an awkward wave.

"Oh, hi," Robyn said back, glancing briefly across, as though she hadn't even realized I was there till now.

"Why don't you help Philippa choose some good colors?" Annie suggested, pushing Robyn in my direction.

"You don't have to if you don't want to," I said. She'd come here to see Annie, not to get stuck with some girl she'd only just met!

"It's fine," Robyn said. She grabbed a couple more books and pointed at a table in the opposite corner from Mom and Dad. "Come on. Let's sit here."

We thumbed through the books in silence for a bit. After a while, I started to feel stupid. I didn't know what to paint, I couldn't decide which colors to use, and now I couldn't think of anything to say, either.

I sneaked a look at Robyn over the top of the books. I could feel myself getting worked up. Why did we have to get saddled with each other? She was the kind of girl I had nothing in common with. I could tell just by looking at her. She probably liked to talk about clothes and makeup and jewelry. Things I had no interest in. I knew the type. They wore the right outfits and had the right friends. I'd learned before not to try to get in with them. It wasn't worth the trouble.

I wished we didn't have to work together. Why couldn't I just sit with my parents?

I tried to look at the books and not to feel awkward about the silence that was sitting between us like a wall.

A moment later, Annie was by our table, and the wall crumbled down.

"Come on, you two — why don't you just grab a couple of mugs and go for it?"

I looked at Robyn. "OK," she said. I followed her silently to the mug shelf.

Robyn picked a china cup with a long, thin handle that tapered daintily down the side. I chose a stocky round one with a big fat chunky handle. It was satisfying and solid to hold. Perfect for hot chocolate. Shame we didn't have perfect hot chocolate to go in it.

Annie was still hovering. "So. What are you going to paint?"

I stared at my mug and didn't reply. What was the matter with me? Just because I had to work with someone who probably had a million things she'd rather do than hang out with me didn't mean I had to turn into a mute. But Robyn seemed to have done the same thing.

"Why don't you just say the first things you can think of?" Annie suggested.

I looked at my chunky mug. "An elephant!" I said after a while.

"Good! Robyn?"

Robyn shrugged. "A giraffe?"

Annie turned back to me.

"A gingerbread house," I said.

"A skyscraper!" Robyn countered.

I examined my mug again. "I know. A forest." I could see it now. Big, thick trees all around it, the sun peeking through. Just like the view out of the

French windows back at the cottage—when you could see it through the rain.

Robyn caught my eye. "OK, and I'll do a jungle."

"Perfect," Annie said, and floated off to join my parents.

We started picking out various shades of green and brown from the paint box. I picked red and orange, too, for the autumn leaves.

"Don't forget blue for the sky," Robyn said.

"You mean gray and white for all the clouds, don't you?"

Robyn laughed. She had a nice laugh—kind of squeaky and shy. I felt myself relax a tiny bit. I realized I'd been too quick to judge her. Maybe I was wrong about her.

"I'm going to make the handle into a rainbow," I said.

"Good idea."

We settled down to paint, working silently, but some of the awkwardness had gone, so it didn't matter quite so much that I still couldn't think of anything to say.

My parents were engrossed in their own mugs. Annie had joined them and chatted easily with them while they worked. There was soft music playing from a stereo behind the counter at the back of the shop. Panpipes or something. Just Mom's kind of thing. I prayed she and Dad wouldn't get up and do a jig. I wouldn't put it past them.

"So, are you here on vacation?" Robyn asked after a while.

I nodded. "Yeah, just for the week." I dipped my paintbrush into the red, then dotted it around the bottom of the mug to make tiny leaves that looked as though they'd fallen on the ground around the trees. "We arrived yesterday."

"Got some good things to do while you're here?" Robyn concentrated on her mug while she talked. She was painting her handle yellow.

"Mom and Dad want to go on a few walks, if the weather improves. They'd like to visit a stone circle near here," I said with a grimace to emphasize it was my parents who liked doing things like that, not me. I didn't want her to think I was even more of a boring wimp than she probably already thought I was. Normal kids of my age aren't usually interested in ancient monuments. They're more into computer games and cell phones.

"Tidehill Rocks?" Robyn said.

"Yes, I think so."

"There's something so magical about a stone circle," Robyn said softly, taking me by surprise. I stared at her.

"What?" she asked, looking up.

"Nothing. It's just . . ."

"Just what?"

I shook my head. "I don't know. Just I wouldn't have expected you to say that." I laughed. "I'm not used to people liking the same kinds of things as me."

Then I thought about Charlotte, and felt bad. She and I had had lots in common. Her parents were just as wacky as mine—more so, probably. They'd proved it by going off to live their "back to nature" life hundreds of miles away.

But there were differences too—and they were bigger than the similarities. Like when the most incredible thing happened to me and I tried to tell Charlotte about it, and all she could do was laugh and thank me for telling such good jokes.

Robyn would probably laugh at something like that, too. I stiffened and got on with my painting.

"We're going to go swimming, too," I said after a while, just to show her we did normal things as well. "Mom and Dad promised to take me to the pool inside the fancy hotel up the road."

Robyn nodded and got back to her mug. "Good idea, if this rain keeps up," she said, glancing up at the window. The rain still spattered against it.

"Anything else we should do while we're here?" I asked.

"There are some great forest walks. The woods have got sculpture trails — there's some amazing stuff. You should definitely check them out if you like walking."

"Great — thanks. A sculpture trail sounds just like my parents' sort of thing," I said, dipping my paintbrush in water. I didn't want to admit I liked the sound of a sculpture walk, too. After all, she was only telling me the local tourist attractions, not what *she* liked to do. I imagined she liked going to the nearest big town and spending the day shopping with her friends. She probably had hundreds of best friends.

"Yeah, it's my sort of thing, too," Robyn said, and I wanted to kick myself for being a coward. What was the matter with me? Hadn't I learned the hard way that it was best to be myself? If people didn't like me for who I was, that was *their* problem. I shouldn't pretend to be someone I wasn't.

It was looking more and more as though my initial impression of Robyn was completely wrong! I tried to think of something else I could say, to show Robyn that I liked the same things that she did. My mind went blank, so I continued painting my mug in silence.

After a while, Robyn held up her mug. "Hey, Annie!" she called. "What do you think?" She'd painted a snake on the handle, twisting around and around, its forked tongue sticking out over the top of the cup.

"I think it's great!" I said shyly.

Annie got up from my parents' table and came over to join us. "Good work there, kid," she said with a smile. Then she turned to look at mine. "Beautiful trees, Philippa. And a rainbow on your handle — what a lovely idea! You're quite gifted."

I blushed instantly. *Me? Gifted? I don't think so!* "Mom and Dad are the talented ones in our family," I said.

"That's not what I've heard," Annie said with a wink. "I believe it was your talent that got you here in the first place."

I glanced across at Mom and Dad. Did they have to tell our life story to everyone they met?

"Oh. Yes, well, I guess so," I said, my face heating up as Annie left us again.

"Your talent got you here—what does that mean?" Robyn asked.

"Oh, it was just a competition at school," I mumbled, embarrassed and shy. "Nothing major—don't worry." I got back to my forest mug and continued working in silence, making a point of concentrating hard so she wouldn't ask any more questions.

I was just putting the finishing touches to the handle when I looked up and saw a man at the window. He was thin and tall, his face pale and taut, dark hair plastered to his head with rain. He didn't have a coat on, just jeans and a black sweater that was drenched and hanging off him. Rain ran down his cheeks as he looked into the shop. Then his eyes fell on Robyn. A moment later, the door was open.

"Robyn! Home—now!" he thundered from the doorstep.

Robyn's face jerked away from her mug. "Dad! What are you —"

"*Now*, I said!"

Annie was out of her seat in a moment. "Martin, there's no need to stand in the doorway. Come in while you —"

Robyn's dad didn't budge from the step, and he didn't look at Annie. It was as though she weren't there. "Robyn, I'm not going to tell you again. You're coming home now!"

Annie shook her head. "It doesn't have to be like this," she said softly, touching his arm. "Martin, please."

Robyn's dad snatched his arm away as though it had been burned. "I'm *waiting*," he said to Robyn, his voice fierce and thick.

Robyn's face had turned bright red. "I'd better go," she said, jumping up from her seat and pulling her apron off.

I tried to hide my disappointment. I'd only just started to get to know her. "Maybe see you again, later in the week?" I said.

"Yeah, maybe," Robyn said quickly.

"Are you going to make me wait out here in the rain all day?" her dad asked, his voice deep and kind of hollow. The way he spoke to her and looked only at her, it was as if he and Robyn were the only people in the world, as if he couldn't even see anything else — or didn't care to. Even my parents had begun to look awkward at his outburst, and they were normally completely clueless about basic skills like how to behave appropriately in public — so he must have been bad!

"I'm sorry," Robyn mouthed to Annie. A second later, she was gone. I watched them leave in the rain, Robyn's dad storming down the road, holding tightly on to her hand as she ran to keep up with his angry strides.

Annie stood at the window till they'd gone out of sight. Then, as if suddenly remembering she had a shop full of people, she smoothed down her apron, tucked a loose hair under the headband, and took a deep breath.

Her face was as flushed as Robyn's had been. "Sorry about that, everyone." She tried to smile, but it was obvious that she wasn't happy. Her eyes didn't crinkle up the same way as they had before. "Now, who needs some help?"

She hovered around us all, flitting between us

like a butterfly, making jokes and talking nonstop, acting as though nothing had happened. I couldn't concentrate on my mug anymore. All I could think was: What on earth *had* just happened?

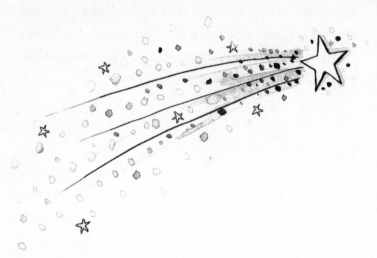

I could feel anger rise inside me as I fluttered around the outside of the cottage. How dare they treat me like this! I'd done my job brilliantly—again—and they weren't even going to let me see her. Or they *might*. They *couldn't make any promises!*

Well, that wasn't good enough for me. They weren't the only ones who had promises to keep. What about the promise of friendship? Didn't that count for anything?

It just wasn't fair. I'd managed to get her to come all the way here, and I was expected to sit around, not knowing whether I could see her or not. I simply wasn't going to let that happen. I *had* to do something. If I could just get in the house.

The windows were all closed; no way in. What could I do?

"Well, that was fun, wasn't it?" a voice boomed from the bottom of the drive. I spun around to see who it was.

Philippa's dad! He was talking as they all made their way up to the house. I quickly flew out of sight. Now what? Perhaps I could fly in when they opened the door. No, too risky. If they spotted me, it could give the whole thing away—and I didn't even want to *think* about how much trouble I'd be in if that happened!

"Philippa, don't forget to take your shoes in," her mom said. "What are they doing out here, anyway?"

"Oh, I decided to change into my boots and just didn't remember to bring them in," Philippa said.

I suddenly had an idea. Her shoes were in front of the door! If I could just get to them. . . .

"Hey, look over here," Philippa's dad said.

"What?" Philippa and her mom glanced over.

"Those trees in the field across the road. All twisted and gnarled. Looks like they've been in a fight," he said with a laugh.

They were all looking away. I had a chance! I could do it now!

I flew over to Philippa's shoes, fluttered my wings over them. Would it be enough?

I'd have to hope so. They were coming back. I shook my wings over the shoes one last time, then turned and flew out of sight.

chapter four
REUNION

We spent the afternoon back at the cottage playing Scrabble. Two *T*s, an *S*, and a *G* were missing, so we had to make some letters out of cardboard. It took the mystery out of the game a little, especially if you had a word like *sting*, but it was better than sitting and watching the rain.

"It's got to stop at some point," Mom said, glancing out the window as she placed her tiles on the board. "*Heart,*" she said. "On a double word. That's sixteen."

Dad wrote down her score, then went back to frowning at his letters. I sat twitching in my seat —

partly out of boredom and partly because something was tickling my foot. It felt as if there was something in my shoe, tickling my toes. I reached down to pull my shoe off so I could scratch my foot.

"Phewey, what's that smell?" Dad said with a wink.

"I've got something in my shoe." It felt like sand. Where had that come from?

Mom got up to poke the logs, ruffling Dad's hair on her way past him. Dad had lit a fire when we came in, and it was starting to die down. "Tell you what," Mom said. "You choose what we do tomorrow, and we'll do it whether it rains or shines."

"Maybe we could go swimming?" I said, putting my shoe back on and wiping the sandy grains on my sleeve.

"Grand idea," Dad said, shuffling the tiles on his rack. "If it's raining, anyway. I imagine you'll want to get out and about if it's sunny, won't you?"

"I guess so," I said. So much for doing whatever I wanted, rain or shine.

To be honest, what I really wanted was to find out where Robyn lived and see if she was all right.

I kept thinking about the way her dad had dragged her out of the pottery shop, how angry he'd been. It made anything embarrassing my parents had ever done seem like small fry.

I wondered if I'd get to see her again while we were here, or if he'd keep her trapped at home for the rest of the week.

As I thought about it and waited for my turn, I snuggled into my chair. The fire was roaring now — so cozy and warm. I closed my eyes. Just for a second. Just to rest my eyelids.

Next thing I knew, I was dreaming. We were playing Scrabble, but the board had disappeared. I had lots of letters on my rack, but as I watched them, they flew off the rack and started spinning around. They were forming a word.

W-I-N-D-O-W.

I started adding up how many points I'd get for it. Two Ws. Didn't they score four points each?

Then more letters came out of nowhere, spinning around my bed.

O-P-E-N.

Before I had a chance to see what the rest of the tiles said, Mom was shaking my shoulder.

I jolted awake. "Sorry!" I said, straightening myself

up in my chair. I looked at my tiles. No Ws. No good letters at all, in fact.

"Come on, dreamer, it's your turn," Dad said, adding *BE* to the *E* from Mom's word. *"Bee!"* he announced. "Five points!" Then he raised his fist like a champion. "Oh, yes! Beat that if you can!"

Mom laughed. "It's going to be a long game," she said.

Going up to bed that night, a quiver ran through me. What if I had another nightmare? I looked at the bed and remembered tossing and turning half the night, the panic and sorrow I'd felt in my sleep. I didn't want to go through all that again.

I read a book until my eyes were so tired the words blurred into black smudges on the page. Switching off the light, I lay looking up at the ceiling, at the feathered charm dangling above me, the shard of glass still lodged in its middle, glinting and winking every now and then as it slowly turned above my head. It was like a hypnotist's pendant waving in front of my eyes, emptying my mind and luring me into a heavy, sleepy state. "You are in my power. . . ."

Soon I couldn't keep my eyes open, and I felt myself drift off to sleep.

So many stairs. How long have I been climbing them? How many are there?

One, two, three . . . six, seven . . . thirteen, fourteen. Have I missed any? There are still so many to go. I keep climbing, and with each step my heart grows heavier.

I can see the room ahead. The door. The light shining from underneath. I've got to get to the light. She's inside. I can see her. My chest heaves with desperation — I can't explain it, don't understand it. All I know is that the

feeling of total aloneness is taking me over, and the only
way I'll ever feel better is if I can get to the light, some-
how get beyond the door, find her. How can I get the door
open? I have to get inside. Please, please let me in!

The light's fading.

No! Don't fade — don't go!

PLEASE!!

I woke up crying silently, my body shaking in the darkness, the feeling of grief and loneliness so fierce it was almost a physical pain.

What on earth was the matter with me? OK, so I'd lost two best friends this year, and I didn't have anyone to replace them — yet. But I would soon. I'd met lots of new girls this semester. Sooner or later, I'd become best friends with one of them. Things weren't that awful. Certainly not so bad that I needed to have terrifying dreams about being deserted!

I tried to talk myself out of the horrible mood the dream had left behind. I thought about what Charlotte would say. She'd probably laugh at me, tell me I was being a drama queen. She'd pull me out of it.

Or would she? Sure, she'd make me feel embarrassed for being so silly, and it would make me want to stop talking about it. But that didn't mean the feelings would go away. Maybe there were some things you couldn't simply laugh out of existence.

I thought about Robyn again. I wondered if she'd understand. Probably not. And I wasn't likely to find out, either. Even if I did happen to see her again this week, you don't exactly go around discussing your innermost thoughts and feelings with someone you've just met.

I turned over and tried to get back to sleep. But my eyes refused to close. It was too dark, too quiet, and I was too scared of what I might dream about. I couldn't bear to feel that awful sadness again.

The charm dangled above my head, twinkling as it turned slowly. Thoughts in my head spun and twirled with it. I was thinking about all the things we'd done today, the shop, the Scrabble game that had gone on for hours. The dream I'd had when I fell asleep in front of the fire.

The dream! Suddenly I was wide awake. The letters — the words. *WINDOW* and *OPEN*. They'd been spinning around my bed — this bed. My imagination was working overtime. Maybe it had been some kind of premonition! A command, something telling me to open my window!

I knew it was just wishful thinking as usual, but I couldn't get the idea out of my mind. And anyway, I was starting to feel hot and claustrophobic. That did it. I got up and opened the window.

As I climbed back into bed, I knocked into the charm spinning above me, and it fell from the beam. Tired and irritable, I grabbed it and shoved it in the bedside drawer.

Please, no more nightmares, I whispered to no one in particular. Then I closed my eyes and fell instantly asleep.

"Philippa."

Someone was shaking my shoulder.

"Philippa," the voice whispered again.

"Mom, please let me sleep a bit longer," I mumbled. "It feels like the middle of the night."

"It *is* the middle of the night," the voice replied. "And it's not your mom!"

I was still dreaming. I must have been, because I knew whose voice that was, and it couldn't possibly be her!

I opened an eye. It *couldn't* be!

I rubbed my eye. She was still there! In front of me, kneeling next to the bed, smiling at me, her green eyes shining in the darkness; her curly blond hair white and frizzy around her head, lit up by the sliver of moonlight tilting in through the window; her wings, soft and delicate, disappearing into her shoulder blades as I focused my gaze on her. It was really, truly her!

"Daisy!" I blurted out.

"Shhh," she said, looking around anxiously. "You'll wake your parents!"

"Daisy!" I said again, trying to whisper. "It's really you! It's really, really you!"

She nodded. "It's really me," she said, standing up and opening her arms wide, as if to show me with a grand flourish that she really had just materialized in my bedroom — after so long without the slightest hint of her.

I was about to leap out of bed and give her a huge hug when I stopped myself. "I'm dreaming, aren't I?" I said flatly. "This isn't real. You're not real, are you?"

"Try me," she said.

What was there to lose? If I was dreaming, at least I was dreaming about Daisy and not about some terrifying grief and a bright light that broke my heart every time I tried to reach it.

I jumped out of bed and threw my arms around her. She felt real! It all felt real!

"You are, aren't you? You're real!" I said. "I'm *not* dreaming!"

"No, you're not dreaming," she replied, and we jumped up and down, spinning in circles as we hugged and laughed.

"I've missed you so much," I said when we'd finally calmed down. I sat on the bed, and Daisy perched on the edge of it. "I thought I'd never see you again."

"I did, too. It's very unusual to see a client twice."

"A client?" I said, my heart plummeting in my chest. Was that how she saw me? After everything we'd gone through together, I was still just a job to her?

"I didn't mean it like that!" she said quickly. "I just mean that once you've done an assignment with someone, that's usually it. You never see them again."

"So how come you're here, then?" I asked. "Is it for another assignment?" I couldn't hide my disappointment that she might be here for work, not because she wanted to see me.

Daisy shifted uncomfortably. "It doesn't matter why I'm here, or why you're here, or anything, does it? Surely all that matters is that we get to see each other again!"

"So you *are* here for a job?"

Daisy ran a hand through her hair and lowered her voice. "Look, I can't talk about it. It's kind of — well, let's just say I managed to mix business with pleasure!"

I couldn't help feeling let down. I didn't want to be "business." I wanted her to be here just because she was my friend. I wanted to hang out together and catch up on everything that had been going on in the last few months.

"I'm in a new department now," Daisy went on. "They're being really strict with me, so I have to be careful." She scurried over to the window and looked out before closing it behind her. "I'm taking a huge risk just by being here — but I had to see you!"

"Really?"

"Of course, really! You're my best friend, and I haven't seen you for months. I've missed you like crazy."

Daisy had called me her best friend! I tried to

conceal a smile, but I don't think I did it very well. The disappointment melted away. "I've missed you, too!" I said.

Daisy smiled, and her cheeks turned pink. "Tell me things!" she said. "What have you been doing? How have you been? I want to know everything!"

I thought about the last few months. I hadn't really done much at all that felt worth reporting. "Been to school, done some magic in the tree house — that's about it," I said, adding silently, *and had no one to share any of it with.*

"How are the tricks going?" she asked.

I shrugged. I didn't want to talk about my magic tricks. I wanted to know about her. "What have *you* been doing?" I asked. "I'm sure it's been much more interesting than my boring old life!"

"Well, I've got this new job," she said. "But I really can't talk about it." She made a face. "I wish I could. I've been wanting to tell you all about it."

"How long have you been in the new department?"

"Just since the summer," she said. "As soon as I got the job, I wanted to tell you. I wanted to see you. I'd been trying to work out a way for ages — and then something came up without me even planning it!"

"What do you mean? What happened?"

Daisy looked over her shoulder, as though checking that no one was there — even though she'd closed the window. She lowered her voice. "I shouldn't tell you," she said. "You know my assignments are top secret. And this one is even more so. But I want to share everything with you!"

"I won't tell anyone," I promised, lowering my voice to a whisper like hers.

She paused, as if she was weighing whether or not to tell me. Then she said, "I came to your house once. It was a special mission."

"Really? When? I never saw you!"

Daisy shook her head. "You wouldn't have recognized me. I wasn't like this."

"As a fairy?" I asked.

She shook her head again. "You know how every time I start a new assignment, I begin as something from nature; like last time, I was a daisy?"

"Yes. So you mean you're something different now?"

She looked over her shoulder again and nodded quickly.

"And you can't tell me what it is?"

"No."

"But that was what you came to me as?"

Daisy nodded. "Listen, I can't tell you any more. I'm sorry. The consequences in this department are really strict. I've been hearing of some terrible things that have happened to fairies in Triple D."

"Triple D?" I said. "What's that?"

Daisy flushed bright red. "Oh, no!" she said. "Look, I didn't mean to say that. You didn't hear that, OK? Please, promise me—don't tell anyone!" Her voice shook. She was looking really scared now.

"Don't worry," I said. "How can I tell anyone if I don't even know what it means?"

Daisy let out a breath. "I'm sorry," she said. "I *want* to tell you all about it. Just I'll get into such trouble."

"What's it to do with? Give me a clue! Twenty questions," I begged, trying to lighten the situation up a bit. I'd never seen Daisy look scared like that.

She laughed nervously. "I can't tell you. It's not like last time. There are lots of us in Triple D, and it's pretty intense. I only get a little time off each night. I really wanted to see you, though. I tried last night, but the window was closed."

The window! The dream! Had Daisy had something to do with—

"Look, I have to go," she said.

"I'm so glad you came!" I said. She gave me a quick hug and headed for the window. "Go back to sleep," she said. "Don't tell anyone you've seen me."

"Of course I won't!"

And with that, she lifted the latch, jumped up onto the windowsill, climbed out into the darkness, and disappeared into the black night.

I woke early. It was just beginning to get light. A grainy gray light filtered in through the window and across the room.

I felt as though I'd been dredged up from the bottom of the ocean, or from the center of the earth. My whole body sagged with heaviness. I wasn't ready to be awake yet.

And then I remembered what had happened last night!

Daisy had really been here, in this room. I'd seen her with my own eyes, even talked to her. Would she come back? Or would that be all I'd see of her for another six months?

I was wide awake now, my mind spinning with thoughts and questions.

I glanced at the clock on my bedside table. It

wasn't even six o'clock. Mom and Dad would sleep for hours.

But I couldn't stay in my room any longer, couldn't even stay inside. I had to get out of here. I got out of bed and bent down to look out my window. The sky was just waking up, growing from black to smudgy deep blue, with a couple of wispy pink clouds hovering in the distance.

I pulled on my clothes from yesterday and crept backward down the wooden steps. Stopping to listen outside Mom and Dad's room, I heard their matching soft snores. That decided it. They were fast asleep. I was getting out of here.

Gently closing the gate behind me, I set off into the woods and along a path that led directly from the garden into the forest.

My feet squished into the soft ground as I dodged puddles that yesterday's rain had left behind. The slurp of my feet was the only sound — apart from the birds, who seemed to be just waking up, too. At first, there was just a tweet or two, as though one of the birds was on lookout duty, telling the others, "Come on, time to get up. Someone's coming!"

As I got deeper into the forest, the birdsong magnified. Soon, there were birds singing everywhere. Long, tuneful riffs repeated over and over; sharp bursts of tinny trills; beep-beeps like car alarms. The forest was a feathered orchestra!

The songs, the thin scrapings of pink clouds high above the trees growing into a promise of sunshine, the trees stretching high into the sky all around me, the damp dewy smell of bark — all of it soaked into me and lifted my spirits till I wanted to laugh with pleasure. And I'd gotten Daisy back, too! Life was great!

I took deep breaths and swung my arms as I walked deeper and deeper into the forest. Mom had told me about doing this after she'd been on a yoga retreat once. It was something about getting oxygen into your body. All the trees would be giving off oxygen, and the more I swung my arms around, the more I'd help it to circulate through my body and release any trapped feelings of anxiety or tension. Something like that, anyway.

It was hard to remember all my mom's words of wisdom, since she had been on about a hundred strange hippie retreats and always came back with some new guide to life. "Follow your inner moonlight; don't hide the madness" was her latest motto. She'd gotten it from someone on an anti-fur protest and had written it on Post-it Notes and stuck them all over the house. I didn't have a clue what it meant, but it seemed to make her happy, so I didn't complain.

I swung my arms wider, shaking off the night's horrible dream and shaking away my questions about whether I'd see Daisy again. Of course I would. I had to!

As I quickened my step, I felt my mood lift even more. The pink streaks in the sky had deepened and lengthened, stretching all around the forest. Red scars joined them, weaving wiggly lines in between the pink. I watched the sky as I walked, twigs cracking beneath my feet. Until . . .

The path — it had gone!

I spun around. Where was it? I must have wandered off it a while ago.

A cold feeling snatched at me, like a freezing hand grabbing my chest from the inside.

It couldn't be far away. I'd only been out here for — how long? I had no idea. I'd left my watch in my room.

I started to walk back in the direction I'd come

from. At least, I *thought* it was the direction I'd come from — but then it looked pretty much the same everywhere.

Stay calm. Don't worry. The path can't be far away. I took a few deep breaths and tried to look at the situation rationally. Tried to imagine how Charlotte might look at it. *Be sensible. Be logical. Make a plan.*

OK, I had a plan. I'd take fifty steps in one direction. If that led me back to the path, then I'd keep going; if it didn't, I'd simply turn around, take fifty steps back, and try again in another direction. I'd keep doing this till I was back on the path. Nothing to worry about.

Fifty steps later, I still hadn't found the path. Fifty steps in another direction, and it was the same. And again and again and again. By now, the cold hand inside me had turned into a claw, scratching at my chest and throat.

Think, think. Come on.

I needed a new plan.

Right. A hundred steps in each direction this time. By now, my heart was racing so fast it was louder than all the birdsong put together — the birdsong that only moments ago had been a gentle, comforting tune, raising my spirits and giving me hope.

Now all I could hear was a sky full of squawks and screams. It was as if the birds were laughing at me. Telling one another how stupid I was to have gotten lost in their forest.

Why had I done it? Why had I come out here? The birds were right. I *was* stupid.

I could feel the sobs building up inside me in big lumps of despair and panic. My eyes stung with tears that I was determined to hold back. I wasn't going to give the mocking forest the satisfaction of seeing me cry.

As I walked on, trying new directions and turning back again and again, the trees started to look thicker. They were crowded more closely together, as if holding their secret more firmly to themselves. They stood utterly still and silent — but I couldn't shake the feeling that they moved whenever I looked away.

OK, now I really *was* being ridiculous! My mind was playing tricks on me. I had to just focus on finding a way out of here.

Leaves littered the ground, crinkling loudly as I walked. It seemed to be the only sound. Nothing else was moving in the whole forest. Even the birds had fallen silent. The forest was watching me, every eye on me, waiting to see what mistake I'd make next. Why did everything suddenly look so different? How could I have thought this was a comforting, beautiful morning?

I kept going. The trees were starting to thin out a bit. The ground was lined with fallen branches: long and thin, rows of them scattered everywhere, as though they'd been tossed aside by someone scrambling through them in a hurry.

I clambered over the fallen branches, searching the ground for anything that looked as if it could be a path, trying to convince myself that I was heading in the right direction. Twigs snapped beneath my feet.

And then I saw it. Right in the middle of the trees, as though it belonged in the forest as much as they did. A house.

I stood still, watching it from behind a tree. What did I think it was going to do, jump up and shout "Surprise!"?

It looked so odd, so different from everything else around it. All around me, there was nothing except forest — trees, birds, leaves, mud. And then this, a quaint little house, right in the middle of it.

It was the kind of house you might draw as a little kid. White and square, with two small windows and an oblong door in between and a thatched roof with a chimney sticking out the top.

I looked to see if there was any smoke coming out of the chimney, any sign of life. Nothing. From here, the windows looked completely dark, so I couldn't see inside, either.

There was a wiggly little path leading up to the house. Again, the kind of path you'd draw if you were five. It was lined with a railing on each side, and netting supporting hundreds of flowers. The trees around the house were full of birds and butterflies flying between the branches. The whole thing was unreal; it was like something out of a fairy tale.

I took a couple of steps toward it — and stopped dead. The pretty netting on either side of the path — it wasn't netting at all. It was huge spiderwebs, spreading and stretching all the way up the path!

Dotted about in between the webs, hundreds of black shells hung on wires. Some of them were open, with enormous moths and butterflies hanging from them. Others were closed, like tombs hanging in rows. What were they? *What was this?*

My feet felt like blocks of concrete, fastening me to the ground.

And then I noticed something else. Inside the house, a shadow moved across the window. There was someone inside!

That was when it *really* hit me. I was lost in the middle of a scary forest — and I wasn't alone!

This time there was no logic, no being rational, no counting steps — none of that. This time I let instinct take over. I turned away from the cottage. And then I ran and ran.

Eventually, breathless and exhausted, I saw it — the path! I prayed it was the right one. It could be any path! It might even lead me back to the weird house. But it was the only path I'd seen for what felt like hours, so I decided to take a chance.

My legs ached from the running, and I slowed back to a walk, carefully making sure I didn't take my eyes off the path, even for a second.

Soon, the trees thinned again. I was getting to the edge of the forest. I saw something ahead. Houses! Our cottage! *Yes!* I started to run again, this time from the sheer relief of being back. I'd never been so happy to see anything in my life as I was to see that garden gate!

Then I thought of something else. How on earth was I going to explain myself to Mom and Dad? I was covered in mud that had splattered all over my clothes and face, and I'd been gone for hours. They'd be worried out of their minds. How could I have been so stupid and selfish?

I let myself in through the patio doors. The kitchen was empty.

"Mom?" I called nervously as I went into the living room. "Dad?"

Nothing. They weren't here. They were probably so worried that they'd gone out looking for me. I went upstairs to change into some clean clothes so I could go out into the village and find them.

But as I passed their bedroom door, I heard something.

Nnnnngghhh!

A snore! They were still in bed! I edged their door open. They were both there — Dad on his front, one arm hanging over the side of the bed, Mom on her back, mouth open, snoring noisily.

I closed the door gently behind me and laughed with relief. Running back up to my room, I checked the time on the clock. It was still only eight o'clock. It felt as though I'd been out there half the day!

I whipped off my muddy clothes and tossed them into my laundry bag. Then, realizing I was completely worn out, I crept into my pajamas, lay down on the bed, and fell instantly asleep.

"Philippa, are you awake?"

Mom's voice filtered through a sleepy, foggy haze.

"Mmisthnkso," I said. I opened an eye and scrunched up my face. Mom was leaning over the bed.

"It's nearly noon," she said. "Dad thought we should wake you. It's a lovely day. We thought maybe we'd go out for a nice walk. Go and see the stone circle or something."

"Mmthbnice," I said, forcing my other eye open and rubbing my cheek. It felt hot and creased from the blankets.

"Come on, then, sleepyhead. The day'll be over before you know it."

With that, she left and went downstairs. As I dragged myself out of bed, hot, heavy, and tired, I remembered my earlier escapade in the forest. Had I imagined it? Had it just been another bad dream?

Then I saw my jeans sticking out of the laundry bag. I pulled them out. Mud all over them. I hadn't imagined it, then. At least I wasn't going crazy.

Mom and Dad were both dressed and drinking coffee in the kitchen when I came down.

Dad patted the bench beside him. "Come and give your dad a hug," he said. I sat next to him and snuggled under his arm.

"Whoops—look what I've found!" he said, reaching behind me and tickling my ear. Then he held out his hand. He had a few folded-up bits of paper in it.

"Dad, that's the oldest trick in the world," I said, laughing. However cheesy his tricks were, I still liked him doing them on me. It was thanks to his magic that we were here, really. He'd taught me magic tricks all my life, and it was the magic show I did at the talent contest at school that had won us this trip. Still, the look-what-I've-found-behind-your-ear trick wasn't exactly his most original or impressive.

Dad pointed at the bits of paper. "Check them out," he said.

I took the paper out of his hand.

"Open them up," he said with a grand magician's

flourish, spreading his arms wide as though he'd just released twenty white doves from a hat.

I unfolded the bits of paper. It was three guest passes for the hotel's indoor pool. "Dad!" I exclaimed. "We're going swimming!"

"Yes, indeedy. I went to get them this morning."

I hugged him again. "Thank you!" I said, kissing him on the cheek. "You're the best dad in the world."

Mom got up to fix some more coffee. "It's a gorgeous day. Maybe we should get out in the fresh air first," she said. "We could always save the swimming for when the weather turns bad again — which I'm sure it will, soon enough."

"Fine by me," I said. As long as we got out of the house and I kept my mind occupied, right now I didn't care what we did.

"Philippa! Sweetie!"

Pretty much everyone in the grocery store turned to see who was shouting. It was the woman with the frizzy hair, the orange-and-green baggy pants, and the old and slightly torn T-shirt with a picture of Che Guevara on it. In other words, my mom.

Six months ago, I would have died on the spot if

she'd yelled to me in public like that. I used to be so embarrassed by my parents that I wished for them to be different. But as soon as I got my wish, I realized I loved them exactly as they were!

She came over and held out a couple of sandwiches. "Tuna mayo or ham and tomato?"

I took her hand. "I don't care. You choose," I said.

"Right. Tuna mayo it is," she said, grabbing three bags of chips and throwing them in the basket with the sandwiches.

As we left the shop, Mom swung my arm while we walked along.

"Isn't that the girl from yesterday?" she said, nodding toward the bookshop in the center of the village. Robyn was kneeling in the window, putting some books out on a stand. She didn't see us at first, but she looked up as we passed by and immediately stood up and waved.

"Let's go and say hello," Mom said.

"Mom, she probably won't want to—" But she was halfway through the door, dragging me along behind her.

"Hi," I said awkwardly as I closed the door behind us.

Robyn came over to the front of the shop. "I'm glad you came in," she said. "I wanted to apologize for yesterday."

"It's fine. Don't worry about it," I said, trying to sound as though seeing someone get dragged out of a shop by a man who looked like a walking explosion was the kind of thing that happened every day.

Mom wandered off. "I'll just have a look around while you girls chat," she said, leaving me stranded and once again not knowing what to say.

"Is this your shop?" I managed eventually, silently screaming at myself for being so dull.

Robyn nodded. "Yeah. My dad's had it for years. We live here, too. We've been in the apartment upstairs since—" She stopped and looked down. Her face seemed to close over and darken, as though a cloud had sailed across it. "Well, for nearly a year," she said quietly.

An awkward silence fell. I glanced over at Mom. She was wandering around the shop, head bent sideways as she scanned the spines of the books.

"Come and sit down for a minute," Robyn said, leading me through the rows of books. They were stuffed into every tiny space you could find, stacked so high in some places I was amazed they balanced.

Her dad was kneeling on the floor, sorting through a boxful of books and making some notes on a pad. He looked up as we passed him and gave a slight nod. I smiled in reply, but he'd looked away again, and I felt like he hadn't even noticed me. It was as though he'd looked through me.

Robyn led me to an alcove at the side of the shop. It had a bay window with cushions and beanbags and an old sofa. A cabinet held rows of comic books, art and craft manuals, magazines. "This is where I go when I want to escape from the world," Robyn said, plunking herself down on a beanbag and patting the one next to her for me to join her.

Her dad had gotten up and started slotting books onto the shelves. I watched him mechanically squeezing them in.

His face was stubbly where he hadn't shaved. His sweater was stained, and one of the cuffs was torn. His jeans looked as worn as his eyes. His black hair flopped onto his face as limp and lifeless as the rest of him. It was as though he didn't care what he looked like. He didn't seem so scary today. More sad and pathetic, to be honest.

He stopped for a moment when he reached the shelves in front of us. "You know, I'm sure your friend has better things to do than hang around here all day," he said.

"Oh, I don't mind," I said. "I like it here."

He nodded vaguely and went back to the box of books.

"Sorry about my dad," Robyn said in a quieter voice. "He's OK, really. He's just never really been the same since . . . Well, he's not always good at being sociable, but he's all right once you get to know him."

I couldn't imagine ever wanting to get to know him! "It's OK," I said. "I'm always having to apologize for my parents, too."

As if on cue, Mom appeared in front of us with a couple of battered-looking novels in her arms. "Ooh," she said, glancing over at a counter she hadn't noticed. "I'll just check out the Climates and Ecology section, and then we'd better get going. Your dad'll be wondering where we are."

Robyn and I dragged ourselves out of the bean-bags and joined Mom at the register.

Robyn's dad put the books in a paper bag. "So, you're here for the week?" he asked without looking up, as though he knew he should be polite but couldn't be bothered to do it properly.

"Yes." Mom beamed in her usual oblivious way. "We're staying just down the road from here. Forest Reach," she said. "It's such a pretty little cottage. Do you know it?"

Robyn's dad froze. He opened his mouth to reply but stopped. The register stood open, like his mouth.

For a moment, Robyn looked shocked, too. Then she hurried to join him behind the counter. She took Mom's change out of his hand and passed it to her, closed the register, and slipped her hand into her dad's.

He looked down at Robyn, staring at her as though he was trying to see something, as though he was lost and she was his only way out.

"Philippa and her parents are on vacation," she said, trying to bring him back into the moment, remind him where he was. "They were thinking of going out walking this week, weren't you?" she said, glancing at me, her face half apologetic, half pleading.

"We thought we'd go to the stone circle, and maybe go swimming one day," I replied, hoping I wasn't going to say the wrong thing. What was the matter with him?

Her dad looked at me for a moment. And then, as

quickly as it had come, the moment snapped away. "Of course, of course. Lovely," he said. "Tidehill Rocks?"

"That's right," Mom said. "Do you know them?"

Robyn's dad coughed and shook himself. "Good choice," he said. "And there are some nice forest walks, too. Especially this time of year." I noticed him grip Robyn's hand as he spoke.

"Robyn mentioned sculpture trails," I said.

"Ooh, that sounds nice," Mom chirped. "Hey, that's a thought. Robyn, would you like to come with us?" She glanced at Robyn's dad. "I mean, if she — if you don't mind."

"Mom, I'm sure Robyn doesn't want to —"

"Can I?" Robyn asked, looking up at her dad. "I mean, it's OK if you need me. I'm happy to stay here if you want me to help."

He shook his head. "It's fine," he said gently.

He looked across at me and Mom as if he'd just remembered we were there. "Robyn told me she met you yesterday," he said. "I'm sorry I didn't get a chance to say hello properly. I'm Martin Fairweather." He held out a hand to Mom.

Mom doesn't really do handshaking. Too formal

for her, but she reached across and gave his hand a floppy wobble, anyway. "Jenny Fisher," she said with a warm smile.

It seemed we'd all decided to pretend to go along with the idea that he hadn't had the chance to say hello yesterday, rather than acknowledge the fact that we all saw him scream his head off at Robyn, flatly refuse to set foot in the shop, and then drag her home.

Robyn's dad turned to me, then back to Mom. "You promise you'll look after her?"

"Of course we will," Mom said. She grabbed a pen from the counter and tore the edge off her paper bag. Scribbling a number down, she shoved it across to him. "Look, here's my cell. If you need anything or want to check anything, just call."

"Dad, I'll be fine," Robyn said.

"It'd be nice to have a guide who knows her way around the forest," Mom said, smiling at Robyn.

Wouldn't it just? I thought, shivering as I remembered my last experience there and wondered for a second if I was really ready to face it again.

Mr. Fairweather gave Robyn's hand a squeeze. "Go on, then. Be careful," he said. "Don't stray from the paths." He took Robyn's face in his hands, looking into her eyes. "You hear me?" he said somberly. "You know what I mean."

Robyn nodded. "I won't, Dad. I promise."

Their eyes locked in a secret deal. What was *that* about?

"Right. OK, then," Mr. Fairweather said. "And make sure you do whatever Mr. and Mrs. Fisher say."

"I will!" Robyn called. Then she ran to the back of the shop. "I'll just get my things," she said. "Meet you outside your house in ten minutes?"

"Great," I said.

Mom and I headed back to the grocery store to buy an extra sandwich for Robyn, then walked home arm in arm, singing "Here Comes the Sun." Mom said it might help guarantee a good afternoon. As far as I was concerned, the fact that Robyn was coming with us had already done that.

"It was nice that your dad let you come out with us," I said as we walked through the woods, kicking up cornflakey bundles of leaves with every step.

Mom and Dad were up ahead, studying a guide to the forest trails that Mom had picked up at the store. Turned out it was easy to find your way if you just looked out for the colored way-markers. We were doing the red path; it was about four miles long, with twenty sculptures along the way. I had no intention of stepping a single inch off the path!

"He's not normally like he was yesterday, you know," Robyn said.

I kicked a huge pile of leaves; they crinkled and crackled as I tossed them in the air, trying to think of a response.

"He's just a bit overprotective," she added before I'd managed to think of a reply.

Overprotective seemed a very generous way to describe the ogre who'd stood shouting on the doorstep of the pottery shop yesterday. I was trying to think of a polite way to say that when Robyn changed the subject. She had a way of doing that. Like she'd say something real and meaningful, then shut the door immediately, and I didn't know how to get in again.

"Look." She pointed down the hill. "Sheep!" I followed where she was pointing. Four wooden sheep sculptures stood, fat and chunky, bent over as if grazing on the forest floor.

"They're great!"

"And look up there." Robyn pointed above us. An enormous beehive, almost the same size as me, sat on a branch in one of the trees.

As we walked, Robyn pointed out the other sculptures. Mom spotted a few, too, jumping up excitedly and squealing at the top of her voice as though she'd just discovered Antarctica. They fitted into the forest so neatly you could look straight past most of them without realizing. And yet once you'd noticed a sculpture, you wondered how you could have missed it in the first place.

They were so random. A wild boar standing on a fence, a kite tangled in a tree, three giant dragonflies sitting on a chair. But there was something about every sculpture that felt utterly natural, too; it was as though each one was as much a part of the forest as the trees and the birds.

That was when I realized. The house I'd seen that morning — it must have been one of the sculptures!

"Where's the one of the house?" I asked.

Robyn looked at me blankly.

"The — the house. It's like a fairy-tale house, out of Hansel and Gretel or something." We'd caught up with Mom and Dad, and I grabbed the guide from Mom. "Hang on — I'll check," I said, scanning the list of sculptures for one that sounded like it could be the house.

Robyn looked over my shoulder. "I can't think of one like that," she said.

There was nothing in the guide that fitted. "Are they all listed here?"

"I think so. I'm not sure. What was it like?"

"Weird. Spooky! The kind of house where a magical, creepy character out of some horror film might live. They'd lure you in with sweets and promises, and once inside, you'd be trapped forever."

Robyn laughed. "You sure you didn't dream it?" she asked.

Suddenly I *wasn't* so sure. I wasn't sure of anything. I couldn't even really remember why I'd found the house so scary. It probably had more to do with the fact that I'd been lost and alone in the forest than anything else.

I passed the leaflet back to Mom, and we continued walking. "You know when you were little and you drew pictures of a house? It's like that. Cute and square and kind of perfect. But it's got a path," I said with a shiver. "A really creepy path with things on it."

Robyn stopped walking. "Oh! Nets and webs and cocoons?"

I shivered. So it *was* real. It *did* exist. I hadn't imagined it! "That's the one," I said.

"That's not a sculpture!" she exclaimed.

"It's not? What is it, then?"

"That's Annie's house!"

chapter six

THE BOY AND THE BUTTERFLY

Annie lives in that strange house in the middle of the forest?" I said as we made our way along the path. "That's a little weird, isn't it?"

Robyn lifted a shoulder in a semi-shrug. "I don't know. She's always lived there, so it seems normal to me. She says she likes seeing lots of people in the mornings at the shop, but she always closes up by lunchtime and spends the rest of her time at home. She likes to be able to escape."

"But all that stuff outside her house—it's kind of spooky."

"She says it's just nature, and everything in nature has a role in creating the beautiful world we live in."

"Sounds like the kind of thing my mom might come up with," I said, although for a split second, I wondered if it was more the kind of thing Daisy might say. Fairy godmothers always come from nature, and they're here to do good—so perhaps the spiderwebs and the coffinlike cocoons weren't as menacing as they looked. They might all be fairy godmothers in disguise!

Yeah, right. Imagination on overdrive again!

Just then, Mom turned up between us. "Girls, look—let's eat!" she said, linking an arm with each of us and skipping toward a café that was just ahead.

She and Dad went inside to get some coffee, leaving Robyn and me outside on our own. We sat down at one of the wooden tables.

I passed a bag of salt-and-vinegar chips to Robyn, and she opened them and munched slowly. There were so many things I wanted to ask her about. The more I talked to her, the more full of surprises she seemed to be.

"Go on, ask me," she said without looking up.

She opened her sandwich and spread a line of chips inside. "I know you want to."

"You're right," I said, secretly pleased that she'd done the mind-reading thing. "I just don't know where to begin."

Robyn looked up. Her eyes were heavy and dark. "Shall I start with my dad?"

I nodded and looked down at my lunch. I wanted to do the thing she'd just done with her chips, but I didn't want her to think I was copying, so I just took a bite out of my sandwich and tried to chew quietly.

"I don't even know why I'm telling you this," she said, shaking her head. "I mean, I hardly know you."

"So why are you?" I asked.

She thought for a moment. "You're different from the other girls I know. I just feel like I can talk to you, like I can trust you."

"You can," I said, realizing that perhaps being different from everyone else can be a good thing sometimes.

She paused, then seemed to make up her mind.

"OK. The reason my dad got all weird earlier

was because of where you're staying," she said. I kept chewing and waited for her to continue.

"We used to live there," she said, so quietly it was almost a whisper; it could almost have been the wind whistling softly past us. "But then we couldn't bear to stay there any longer, surrounded by memories. So Dad sold it, and we moved into the apartment." She paused a beat before adding, "After my mom died."

"Oh, Robyn," I said. "I didn't know. I'm—gosh, how awful." I stammered. I didn't have a clue what to say.

Robyn waved a hand and tried to smile. "It's OK," she said. "It was nearly a year ago. A year ago on Saturday, in fact."

"I'm really sorry," I said, feeling stupid and inadequate.

"My dad took it really badly. I mean, I did too. At first it was just so awful. I was a wreck—but then something changed. I don't know why, really. It was practically overnight. I guess I just kind of switched off." She glanced up at me. "I feel guilty about it sometimes. I think I should be more upset, more like I was at the beginning. I just can't cry—I haven't cried since just after it happened. But it feels like the tears are still there; it's like they're kind of stuck inside me. Does that make sense?"

I nodded. It did make sense. It explained what I'd seen in her eyes. A line of tears just behind her eyelids, like an army that wouldn't advance but wouldn't let you get past, either.

Robyn shook her head. "You wouldn't believe it if I told you what my dad used to be like," she said with a rueful laugh. "He was always smiling, like my mom. Just being around them made everything feel warm and safe. I never knew anything bad could happen. D'you know what I mean?"

"Yeah," I replied, glancing over at my parents. Mom had a piece of cake on her plate, and as I looked over, Dad pointed at something on the ceiling. The second Mom looked up, he stole a bite of her cake. Mom squealed and tickled him in reply, the pair of them giggling like kids. "I know exactly what you mean," I said.

Until this year, when Charlotte had moved away and Daisy had done her assignment and left, I'd never really known anything bad could happen, either. Anything that involved losing someone.

"Dad's just never been the same. It feels like

he's not quite there most of the time. He hardly notices the world around him, and he doesn't care about things like he used to. He wanders around the place like a ghost, he dresses like a bum, he doesn't wash his hair, and he hardly makes an effort with the customers. It's like he's given up on everything."

"Except you," I said.

"Well, yes, I guess. But everything else — it's just a mess. The shop's in chaos. I've even started trying to help with the accounts now. He doesn't notice it all building up around him, and it worries me. It's getting out of control."

"Can you talk to him about it?"

Robyn shook her head. "He won't. He's so stubborn. He doesn't go out, doesn't see anyone socially. I'm the only person he talks to at all, and even then — well, there are certain things we never talk about."

"Your mom?"

She nodded. "It's like he just can't. And neither can I. We both spend all our time pretending it's not there, acting as though there's nothing wrong. And yet I know it's the only thing either of us ever really thinks about."

Robyn took a bite of her sandwich. "We both pretend life is OK; we act as though we're coping, but I think both of us are surrounded by a black hole so big we can't see beyond it. Sometimes I try. I ask him about Mom, or mention her name, or just want to look at photos or something. But he stops me. It's as if he doesn't dare even let me try to get across the blackness. I think he's scared I'd fall into it and never get out."

I didn't know what to say.

"But lately, I've started to feel different again. I think it's because it's coming up to a year now. I've started having bad dreams again. Not as bad as before. Not yet, but I know they're coming — and Dad does, too. They've been getting worse each night. That's why he's even more protective than usual at the moment."

Listening to her made me feel so sad, and I wished I could say something to make her feel better. I searched every corner of my brain for something. Anything.

"I wish I could help," I said feebly.

Robyn twisted her mouth into an attempt at a smile. "Thanks," she said. "But you can't. No one can. My mom used to tell me a story about that. 'The Boy and the Butterfly,' it was called."

"Tell me," I said, putting down my chips and folding my arms.

"You want to hear the story?"

I nodded.

Robyn's eyes went all dreamy and far away. Then she smiled. "OK. So, a young boy was running through a garden when he saw a tiny chrysalis on the path. He stopped to look at it and ended up watching it and waiting for hours."

"What was he waiting for?" I asked.

"He wanted to see it turn into a butterfly. Nothing happened, so he took it home to keep an eye on it. After a few days, the chrysalis quivered! He saw a small opening appear."

"In the chrysalis?"

"It was the size of a dot! But it got bigger. And then he saw something. The butterfly — trying to get out. It was pushing frantically against the surface, as though it was desperate to break free."

"What happened?"

"Nothing. It couldn't get out. After a bit, the butterfly stopped even trying. It seemed to have given up." Robyn's eyes widened as she went on. "So the boy had an idea how he could help. He got some scissors and cut the chrysalis open. And then he waited for the butterfly to spread its wings and fly away. But it didn't. It didn't go anywhere. It couldn't fly at all. The next day at school, he told his teacher what had happened, hoping she could help. She told him that he'd done more harm than good."

"Why?"

"Because the butterfly needed the struggle in order to build up the strength to fill its wings with power. That's how it works. Without that struggle, the butterfly would never fly."

Robyn fell silent. I wanted to respond, show her I understood, but before I had the chance to say anything, Mom and Dad were back at the table with a tray full of desserts.

"Cheesecake, butterscotch pudding, key lime pie, and a chocolate brownie!" Dad announced with a wide grin. "Who's having what? Or shall I just cut each one into four?"

"Minus your share of the cheesecake," Mom said, pinching his cheek. "Seeing as you already sneaked it in the line."

"I don't care what I have," I said, wishing they'd stayed away longer. I wanted to keep talking to Robyn on our own. I wanted to talk about the boy and the butterfly. I wanted her to know that even though I understood what it meant, if there was a way I could take some of her sadness away without clipping her wings, I'd want to try.

"You choose first," I said, pushing the tray in front of Robyn. I knew it wouldn't make anything any better, but it was all I had to offer.

It wasn't until we'd finished lunch and were on our way back through the forest that we got to talk again.

"Sorry for going on and on earlier," Robyn said. "I don't know what came over me."

"Don't apologize. I feel — I don't know, I guess kind of honored that you shared it with me," I said, "if that doesn't sound too stupid."

Robyn smiled. "It doesn't sound stupid at all. It sounds nice. Thank you."

We walked along in silence. It's funny how many different kinds of silence there are. This was one that we were in together, sharing, with everyone else on the outside.

"You know, I haven't talked about my mom with anyone," Robyn said after a while.

"Haven't you got a best friend?" I asked, half hoping she'd say yes, because I didn't like to think of her being lonely, but half hoping she'd say no, because already I liked the idea of being special — even if it was selfish of me to think like that.

Robyn shook her head. "Not really. There's a group of us. We get along really well and hang out together. We go shopping, talk about music and movies and clothes." She made a face.

"What?"

"I don't know — just it's not really me. Sometimes I feel like I'm acting a part that they want me to play. They think that's who I am, so I go along with it. Do you know what I mean?"

I nodded, feeling guilty that I'd thought all those things about her, too.

"I kind of lost two best friends this year," I said. "I could talk to both of them, in different ways. Now I just have friends that I hang out with, and I miss having someone I can share all my secrets with."

"It sucks, doesn't it?"

I thought for a moment. "I know it's nothing like losing your mom, but I think I can understand a little bit about how it feels when someone close to you goes out of your life."

I told her about Charlotte, about how we'd been friends since nursery school, and how I'd been convinced that we'd be best friends for ever, and how it felt as though someone were chopping off a limb when she moved away.

"But the last time I saw her, it was like we were in different worlds — like we'd never even been best friends in the first place."

Robyn nodded. "It sounds horrible."

"It was."

"You said you'd lost two best friends. What happened to the other one?"

I thought about Daisy. I'd only just met Robyn, and even though I felt as if I could talk to her about anything, telling her I'd become best friends with a fairy who'd granted me three wishes was probably pushing it!

"Oh, that was just someone who lived nearby for a while," I lied, trying to sound casual. "She wasn't really my best friend. She didn't stay around long enough."

"But you wish she had?" Robyn asked.

"Yeah," I said. "I do."

I really wanted to talk about Daisy. I had the feeling Robyn would believe me and understand — or maybe it was just a hope. Either way, I didn't want to lose my new friend the moment I'd met her by confessing I was about to turn twelve and still believed in fairies! Well, I didn't just believe in them; I *knew* they were real. But that's not the kind of thing most girls my age would go along with, and even though I didn't think Robyn would laugh at me like Charlotte had done, I couldn't be sure. It wasn't worth the risk.

I decided to change the subject. There was something else I'd been wondering about.

"So how long have you known Annie?" I asked. "You seem really close."

Robyn kicked her way through a huge pile of leaves. "I've known her all my life. She used to be Mom's best friend."

"Your dad doesn't seem to like her very much."

"That's the understatement of the year!" Robyn said with a dry laugh. "Something happened after Mom died. I've never really understood what. One day we were all friends. The next, they had a huge argument and I was almost banned from having anything to do with her."

"That sounds awful."

"It *was* awful. Annie's like an aunt to me. She's always been there. Dad says she's not what she seems."

"What does he mean?"

"I don't know. He won't tell me. Just tells me to keep away from her. So I have to be careful about it when I see her. I know how angry Dad gets about it, and I hate making him angry. He's had enough to deal with in the last year."

"You sound like me," I said.

"How do you mean?"

"Oh, I don't know. Like you're so busy trying to keep everyone else happy that you can forget about yourself sometimes."

"I guess so."

"Wow, look at this!" Mom and Dad had stopped in front of a huge gong hanging between two trees. Drumsticks made from branches were propped up in front of it.

"This is great," Robyn said. "You have to hit the gong, then turn and stand with your back to it for the best effect." She handed me one of the drumsticks. "Try it."

I hit the gong and turned around. I was looking

out across the rows and rows of trees. The sound echoed and vibrated through the trees. It felt like a heartbeat, coming through me and snaking around the whole forest.

"That's completely amazing!" I said when the vibrations had finally subsided.

"Good, isn't it?"

We walked on ahead, standing to the side as Mom and Dad each took a turn at the gong.

"Do you think your dad and Annie will ever be friends again?" I asked, stopping next to a tree while we waited.

Robyn leaned back against the tree beside mine and pulled on a piece of loose bark. "I don't know. He won't even tell me what it's about. I've asked him lots of times, but even mentioning her name gets him angry, so I've given up. I can't imagine what she's done. All she ever did was be a friend to Mom—to all of us, really. She and Mom were so close they were like sisters."

"Perhaps she reminds him of your mom too much or something."

"I've thought that, too. But I don't think that's it. It's—oh, I don't know."

"What?"

"I don't know. Just, I think there's something more to it. They were OK at first, then he went to see her shortly after Mom died. He came back that night more angry than I've ever seen him. He was like a volcano on the brink of erupting. Things changed after that. He told her she was never to come over again."

"And he stopped you from going to see her?"

"He tried, but I kicked up such a fuss that he finally compromised on that one. I said whatever had happened between them was their business, but he couldn't stop me from seeing her if I wanted to."

"And he agreed?"

"Well, not exactly. He didn't ban me, but he's made it clear he doesn't like it." Robyn grimaced. "As you probably noticed."

"I wonder what they argued about."

"Me, too. All I know is it must have been something really big. It's like he can't forgive her for something. I just don't know what she's done."

"It sounds horrible."

Robyn scrunched up her face as she pulled harder on the bark. "I've gotten used to it," she said.

I wasn't convinced.

"Come on, chatterboxes!" Mom called to us.

They'd finished playing the gong and had set off down the path. We'd been so deep in our conversation that neither of us had noticed.

"Actually, that was kind of a lie," Robyn said as we ambled along, keeping a little distance between us and my parents. I wanted to keep Robyn to myself for now.

"About you being used to it?"

Robyn nodded.

"I thought so."

"You know, sometimes I miss him almost as much as I miss my mom. Does that make sense?"

I thought about Charlotte. "You miss how he used to be, how things used to be between you," I said. "It's like the person you used to know isn't there anymore."

"That's exactly what I mean!" She stopped and stared at me. "You really understand me, don't you?"

"I don't know. I hope so. I'd like to."

"I think you do. I'm not used to it." Robyn started walking again, kicking into a bundle of leaves that someone had piled up beside the path.

"Is that OK?" I asked. "You don't mind?"

"No, it's great," she said with a smile. Then that faraway look crossed over her face again. "My mom understood me—and now she's gone. And Annie gets me—but I hardly ever get to spend time with her."

I didn't have a chance to respond, since we'd caught up with Mom and Dad. Mom was waiting for us on the path; Dad had gone to the edge to take some photos. I didn't realize we'd come so far up.

"Just thought we'd sit down and take in the view," Mom said. "You two can go ahead if you like."

"We'll wait, too," I said. Mom joined Dad on a bench, and we went over to a grassy clearing a little bit away from them so we could keep talking. Below us, we could see the tops of the trees, standing so straight and tall and thin—and bare. Half of them had already lost their leaves; the others still had some from halfway down, like skimpy grass skirts around their middles.

"It's nice talking to you," Robyn said, spreading her coat on the ground so she could sit on it. "Sometimes I guess I just feel lonely."

She leaned back on her elbows and stared up at the

sky, as if she were looking for something long lost. Her eyes were so sad; they were like deep, dark pools filled with all the tears in the world. But they had a kind of hardness too, like a thin sheen of ice lying still on the surface of black water. Thick enough to separate you from what was below, keep it away from you, but thin enough that if you weren't careful you could slip through it and be lost forever.

"Do you believe there's anything up there?" she asked, breaking my thoughts.

Up there? Could I say it? Could I tell her that I believed there were fairies? That I *knew* there were fairies, in a place called ATC? That one of them was the best friend I'd mentioned earlier? I thought again about Charlotte and how she always reacted to me when I talked about anything like that: all the ways that she would prove that my theories were nonsense, how she'd tell me I was bonkers and laugh at me. Most girls my age would do the same. No, I couldn't say anything. I didn't want to run the risk of Robyn thinking I was completely crazy.

"Like what?" I asked with a shrug.

She shrugged back. "I dunno. Heaven?"

Just as well I hadn't said anything, then. Heaven.

Normal stuff! The kind of "up there" people were officially allowed to believe in! Except Mom and Dad had never been big on things like heaven, so I'd never really believed in it, either.

I was about to reply when she added, "Or something?" She turned her sad eyes on me.

"What kind of something?" I asked, holding my breath while I waited for her to reply.

She shook her head. "I really don't know. I get this feeling sometimes — it's so real I can almost touch it. Then it goes away, and I tell myself I imagined it. Dad always tries to laugh it off when I tell him about it."

"Yeah, I know what you mean," I said, thinking of Charlotte again.

She kept staring up at the clouds, as though they might reveal something that would answer her questions. "Do you know what, though?" she said. "I don't believe he really laughs it off. I think he knows something."

"Knows something? What kind of something?"

Robyn let out a long sigh. "I don't know. Sometimes I catch him staring at the sky, and I think he sees it, too."

"Has he ever said anything?"

She shook her head and pulled on the grass. "No way. He never talks about anything except work. He's not going to suddenly start discussing some sort of magical beings in the sky!"

"Is that what you think it is?" I breathed, my hopes raised. Magic! She *did* believe in something — she *would* believe me about Daisy!

Robyn flushed instantly. "Well, no, not really. Not literally, obviously. It's just a turn of phrase," she said. Then she got up and picked up her coat. "Come on," she said, the wall up again with me on the outside. "We'd better get going, or my dad'll start wondering what's happened to me."

I got up and followed along behind her. Mom and Dad had gotten up too, and we set off back along the path. Robyn walked close to my parents, pointing out sculptures and telling them about the birds she'd seen in the forest. I didn't get another chance to talk to her until we were almost at the end of the path. She was still chatting away to Mom and Dad when I'd had enough.

"Robyn, your shoelace is undone," I said.

She stopped to check her boots. Mom and Dad kept on walking.

"It's fine," Robyn said.

She was about to set off when I grabbed her arm. "Wait."

Robyn looked at me. "What is it?"

I shook my head and waited till Mom and Dad were out of earshot, then I let go of her arm and we started walking slowly along. "I need to say something," I said carefully. I'd been thinking about it all the way back, while she'd been talking with my parents about everything she could think of.

Robyn looked down at the path as we walked.

I took a breath. I knew I was taking a risk. I knew I might be putting this brand-new friendship on the line. But I knew something else, too. Something I'd learned from Daisy. I had to be myself. I had to be true to what I believed in, even if it was a gamble.

"Right," I said. Then I coughed and started again. "Look, the thing is, you might be happy to go around pretending all the time, hanging out with friends who don't understand you and don't even try, talking nonstop with my parents to avoid having a real conversation with me. . . ."

Robyn kept looking down, sidestepping a puddle. I walked straight through it without realizing. I didn't care.

"But I'm not. I'm not going to put on an act, OK? I know I've only just met you, but you're the first person I've been able to talk to for ages. Really talk to."

Robyn glanced up at me. "Yeah, you, too," she said shyly.

"And I'm not going to lie and pretend with you, OK?"

"OK," she agreed.

"So. In that case . . ." I took another breath. I felt as if I were poised on a cliff, about to dive into the sea, looking down, checking that it was safe before taking the plunge.

"So, in answer to your question earlier — yes, I do believe there's something up there. OK? I'm not going to brush it aside. And I'm not talking about heaven or anything like that."

Robyn stared at me. "What *are* you talking about, then?"

I closed my eyes. Maybe if I couldn't see her reaction, it would be easier to say it. "Fairies," I said eventually.

Robyn didn't say anything. Eventually I opened my eyes to see her smiling.

"Really?" she asked.

She was laughing at me! This was my last chance to back out, say I was joking.

No! I *wasn't* backing out. I'd be betraying Daisy if I did that, and after everything she'd done for me, there was no way I'd do that.

"Yes, really," I said firmly.

Robyn grinned widely. She was about to burst out laughing! Why had I been so stupid? Just because I believed in fairies—*knew* about them—didn't mean I had to go blurting it out. What on earth was I—

"Me, too!" she breathed. "I've never told anyone before! It's not the kind of thing you can admit, especially once you get to middle school." Her words tumbled out of her in a landslide. "I'd probably be teased for it. But I do—I believe in fairies!"

We'd nearly caught up with Mom and Dad. I wished that we still had hours to keep talking. We'd only just got started!

"Come on, slowpokes. Robyn's dad will be thinking we've kidnapped her!" Dad called.

"I don't just believe in them," Robyn added quickly, her deep brown eyes staring into mine.

They didn't look sad anymore. They looked full of mystery, as though they were so deep you could hide your biggest secret in them and it would never be found.

"I *know* they're real," she said.

"You know it? But how?"

"I saw something once," Robyn said quickly, then she stopped. "Look, I don't know if I can trust you yet. I've never told anyone about this, and you'll think I'm stupid or crazy."

"I won't!" I insisted. "I've told you I believe in them, too."

"I know — I'm just not sure. It sounds so corny and childish."

Before I had a chance to convince her otherwise, Dad had jumped in between us, putting an arm around each of us and making us join in with knock-knock jokes all the way back to the village.

But all the way there, I had just one thought in my head.

What did she know? *What had she seen?*

ATC

"It's going well, wouldn't you say?"

"Definitely. She did a great job. She got the girl here. We've brought them together—and the sharing has begun. Couldn't be better. Well, except . . ."

"Except what?"

"Time. We're running out of days. There's still a lot of ground to cover. If we don't finish the job in time, we might as well not have bothered at all. Our efforts will have been useless. Worse than useless, in fact. If we don't make this happen in time, the results could be catastrophic."

"Don't worry. I know. We have to do this quickly. I just don't know how we can go any faster."

"I've got an idea."

"Go on."

"I've been monitoring Daisy's movements through her MagiCell."

"Yes?"

"And—well, she visited the girl."

"What? She was given strict orders to—"

"I know, I know, but listen. Let's not punish her just yet. The friendship may turn out to be even more useful to us than we'd thought. I've been scrolling through the MagiCell images, and there was something odd on the radar log. I didn't think it was all that important when I first looked. I thought it was just residue because of the room. But I checked again just before coming to you, and now I'm not so sure. The colors have grown and sharpened. I think there's something more to it."

"Show me."

"See that flashing color in the top corner? It's displaying a recognition code for this mission."

"What is it?"

"I don't know exactly, but there's something in the girl's room that could be important to us."

"Program her MagiCell. Find out more. Whatever is in the room, I want it—tonight!"

chapter seven
SPECIAL MISSION

Robyn and I didn't get another chance to talk. Her dad was waiting outside the shop when we got back. I thought he was going to have another outburst—but he didn't. He just looked relieved.

"Hello, darling," he said gruffly, gathering Robyn into his arms and kissing her head. "Did you have a good time?"

"Yeah, Dad," she said, wriggling out of his arms. "How's the shop?"

"Oh, fine, fine, you know." He nodded to Mom and Dad. "Thank you," he said. Then he turned away.

"The girls had a lovely time together," Mom said

to his retreating back. "They didn't stop talking for five minutes."

He half turned back and gave us all a quick smile. "Thanks again," he said.

"Maybe see you again before we go?" I said to Robyn.

"Definitely!" she replied with a grin. It felt like a deal. There was more to be said. More to find out and share. I was desperate to know what she'd meant earlier, what she knew about fairies — and just as desperate to tell her all about my own experiences!

I wondered for a second if it really would be disloyal of me. Was it giving away fairy secrets if I told her about Daisy, ATC, and 3WD?

Surely it couldn't be disloyal as long as I didn't tell her Daisy had been to see me here. Daisy was under orders from her superiors, but I wasn't! I had no idea if she would be able to visit me again, and not being able to talk about her with anyone was driving me crazy. But finding someone else my age who knew fairies existed — well, that was the next best thing to actually being with Daisy!

"Can Philippa come over tomorrow?" Robyn asked her dad as he opened the shop door.

He paused for a moment in the doorway. Turning

back to us, he said, "Well, I don't know. I mean, she's on vacation with her parents. She might not want to spend all—"

"I'd love to!" I said. I turned to Mom and Dad. "Can I? Please?"

"Oh, I'm sure we can manage without you for a few hours, sausage," Dad said with a smile. I tried to pretend he hadn't just called me "sausage" in front of a brand-new friend. *Dad, I'm not six anymore,* I wanted to say. I didn't, though. I never would. I just wished that he would one day figure out for himself the correct way to refer to his nearly twelve-year-old daughter in public. I could feel my cheeks burning. I studied the ground so I could hide them.

"Right. OK, then," Mr. Fairweather said. "We'll see you tomorrow." And with that, he took Robyn's hand and went inside.

We stood in the street for a moment.

"Not the most sociable fellow on the planet," Dad said.

Mom nodded seriously. It didn't bother me, though. I didn't care what Mr. Fairweather was like as long as he'd let me and Robyn be friends.

I spent all evening thinking about what Robyn might

have meant earlier. What did she know about fairies? Had she had an experience with a fairy godmother like I'd had? I wondered which department her fairy could have been from. She might even have had someone from the Three Wishes Department, too. Daisy told me people had to be really unhappy to get a fairy from 3WD, and surely Robyn would have qualified for that. She'd had so much sadness in the last year. Maybe that was it. Maybe she'd even met Daisy! How amazing would that be!

My mind was still spinning with thoughts and questions when I went to my bedroom. As I got ready for bed, I thought about Robyn living in this very house.

Had this been her bedroom? I glanced around, looking for a clue or sign of any sort. There was nothing. The rental agents would no doubt have changed it completely since she'd lived here. But the fact that we were connected by the house as well as everything else made me feel even more excited about our new friendship.

I wished I could tell Daisy about Robyn, tell her there were other girls like me who believed in fairies. I wanted to tell her about the day I'd had and the conversations I'd had. I wanted to tell her about everything, because that's what you do with your best friend.

I opened the window before I got into bed.

Please come in again, Daisy.

I lay in bed, glancing at the window every five seconds. Nothing. Maybe she wasn't coming. She said it was hard to get away.

I tried to stay awake, tried to keep watching, but the fresh air and the walking and all the thinking must have worn me out, and I couldn't stop my eyes from closing.

There was a noise in my room. A creaking sound — it was coming from the window. Someone was there. Someone — or some*thing*. Cold air rushed into the room, brushing over my face, and the curtains whooshed softly.

Then there were sparkles, lights, crackling around me, filling the room with color.

Daisy!

I was wide awake in a flash. There she was! In my bedroom. She was bending over, kneeling on the floor beside my bed; something on her wrist was flashing.

"Daisy?" I whispered, sitting up in bed. She jumped up instantly.

"Philippa!" she said quickly. She ran a hand through her disheveled hair and smiled at me.

"You came back!" I said, grinning widely.

"Of course I did," she said. "Why wouldn't I?"

"I don't know. I guess I—"

"What? Thought I'd forgotten about you?"

I laughed, but then I noticed the way she was smiling. It looked—I don't know. Different. Kind of forced. As though she were hiding something.

"What were you doing just now?" I asked.

"When? Oh, that—I just dropped something," she said. "So, what have you been up to today?" she added, glancing around the room as she spoke. She was different from the last time she'd been here. I couldn't put my finger on what had changed—she just seemed nervous and edgy.

"We've been in the woods," I said.

"We?" She stopped glancing around.

"Me, Mom, Dad, and Robyn."

"Robyn?" she said. "Who's Robyn?"

"She's my new friend. She's great. She lives here, and she came out with us today, and we talked and talked all day. She's the first person I've been able to talk to for ages."

"I see," said Daisy, trying to sound casual and unconcerned.

I laughed. "Daisy, she's not a replacement for you. Surely you know that! You're the best friend anyone could want."

She smiled.

"You're a fairy godsister!" I added.

Daisy's smile fell. "Oh, right. Is that the only reason I'm such a good friend?" she asked.

"No, it's not! It's because you're loyal and brave and strong and daring, and you're fun to be with!"

Daisy's face relaxed into a smile. "OK," she said. "I was just checking."

"It's just nice to have someone I can talk to," I said. I wondered whether to mention what had happened at the end of the day. Should I tell Daisy that Robyn believed in fairies? That she knew something? That I'd told her I knew something, too?

Before I had time to decide, Daisy went all serious again. "Listen, I can't stay long," she said.

"I understand," I said. "You're afraid of getting caught."

Daisy shook her head. "No, it's not that. They know I'm here this time."

"What? How come? I thought you said you'd be in terrible trouble if you got caught."

"I know. But things have changed."

"What do you mean? What things? How have they changed?"

"I can't tell you," Daisy said.

"You can't tell me? More secrets," I said, trying to hide my disappointment. I wished Daisy didn't have to keep so many things secret from me. I wished we could share everything, like real best friends.

Daisy's cheeks puffed out in that way that they sometimes did when she was embarrassed about something. "OK, to tell you the truth, I don't really know," she said.

"You don't know why you're here?"

She nodded. "I have to get something. It's in here, but I don't know what it is."

"Oh." This time I didn't even try to hide my disappointment. She hadn't come back to see me at all! "I understand, I'm just a job—again," I said.

Daisy perched on the edge of the bed. "Philippa, listen. You're not just a job, and you never will be. I just have to do this," she said. "They've hinted that if I do it well, they'll give me some time off when we can actually hang out together before you go home again."

"What is it you have to do?" I asked.

"I've got to find something." She was holding her wrist out. "And I have to get on with it. They told me to be quick." She pressed something on her wrist, and the flashing was there again — the same flashing I'd seen when she first came into my room.

"What's that?" I asked.

"My MMC," she answered, walking around the room and watching the flashing.

"MMC?"

"Micro MagiCell. They have to be tiny in this department," she explained.

Daisy had used her MagiCell — the most important part of a fairy godmother's equipment — to help me make my three wishes earlier this year. It did amazing things, like tell you when the next shooting star was due. That's when all the wishes in the world are gathered up and taken back to ATC. And it could tell you if there was danger approaching and if someone had had a fairy godmother's help before, and all sorts of things.

"What's it telling you?" I asked.

"I'm not sure. Hang on." She held her wrist out, staring at it as she maneuvered around the room, finally stopping at the bedside table. "Got it!" she said. She looked across at me. "What's in here?"

"Nothing," I replied.

Daisy opened the drawer. She pulled out the feathered charm I'd found outside. I'd forgotten about that. "What's this?" she asked.

"Oh, that. It's just a kind of lucky-charm thing," I said, not very helpfully. "I had it hanging on the ceiling, but it fell off, and—"

"Where did you get it?" Daisy interrupted, pressing buttons on her MagiCell while she spoke.

"I—I found it," I said. "It was hanging outside."

Daisy continued tapping buttons. "Yes, this is it," she said, more to herself than me.

"I thought it might help me sleep," I added.

Daisy looked up from her MagiCell. "Why did you need help sleeping?"

I shrugged. "I couldn't sleep very well on the first night. Not that it's done much good. I've had awful dreams pretty much every time I've closed my eyes."

"Since you've had this thing?" Daisy asked.

I thought about it. Now that she mentioned it, the dreams *had* been since I'd had the charm. "Yeah, I suppose so," I said. "Except I was all right last night," I added. *After I'd put it in the drawer!*

Daisy leaned in farther. "It's torn," she said.

"Yeah, that's my fault."

"Your fault?"

"I chipped some of the glass trying to get the window open — it got lodged in the middle."

Daisy tapped some more buttons. "Listen, I need to take this away."

"Why? What is it?"

"I don't exactly know. I just know it's what they want."

"What who want?" I said impatiently. I didn't mean to get angry, but I was beginning to feel that all I was doing was asking questions that Daisy couldn't answer. Or *wouldn't* answer.

"Philippa, I'm really sorry," she said, turning to me. "Look, do you trust me?"

"Of course I trust you," I said, reaching out for her hand. "Always. No one comes close to you."

"Really?" Daisy smiled. "What about Charlotte?"

I shook my head.

"Or your new friend?"

"Robyn?" I said, laughing. "I've only just met her. No, you're my best friend, and if you say you need to do something, then I know you have a good reason for it."

"I have," she said seriously. "I really have. I'm sorry; I just can't tell you more. But I'll tell you everything I can, as soon as I can, OK?"

"It's fine," I said. "Like I said, I trust you."

"Good. I just have to do this, and then I promise I'll come back and we'll do something nice together — whether they say I can or not! OK?"

"OK," I said with a smile.

She started to leave.

"Will you come back at night, or can we actually spend a day together?" I asked.

"It depends on whether they let me see you or if I have to sneak out again, like last night. It's really hard to get away during the day," she said. "It's different from my last assignment. We have to stay in our form that we take from nature during the day."

"Daisy, at least tell me that. Tell me what you are, what you transform from."

Daisy looked around one last time. She even

checked outside the window and behind the curtains before replying. Then she leaned close and indicated to me to do the same.

"OK, I'll tell you," she said. "I'm a butterfly."

"A butterfly!" Daisy was a butterfly! That was so cool! "Wow! Do you get to fly around all over the place?"

Daisy stared at me. "Philippa, I do that anyway. I'm a fairy!" Then she burst out laughing. After a moment of wondering how I could have been so stupid, I started laughing, too. At first, just a giggle slithered out, but the more I thought about it, the funnier it seemed. I kept seeing her face creased up with laughter, and it made me laugh even more. Soon we were both rolling on the floor laughing like lunatics, hands clapped over our mouths so we wouldn't make too much noise and wake my parents, tears rolling down our cheeks.

"You're a butterfly," I kept saying. "You can fly!" And we'd both burst out laughing again.

Then I had a thought. I stopped laughing. "You're a butterfly," I said slowly, thinking about her as a butterfly, picturing her — I could see her now.

Daisy was looking at me, tears of laughter in her

eyes as she waited for the punch line. When it didn't come, she said, "I can fly!"

But I didn't laugh this time. I sat up. "What color are your wings?" I asked.

"What do you mean? You've seen them. They're—"

"No, I mean as a butterfly." I shut my eyes and tried to remember. It had been so distinctive, I'd never seen one like it before or since. "Have they got dark purple edges? And—what was it? Pink circles, I think?"

Daisy stared at me, her mouth open. Then she nodded silently.

"I knew it!" I said, jumping up. "You made us come here! You came to my house and landed on the map. You did, didn't you?"

Daisy stared at me in silence a bit longer. When she spoke, her voice was a hoarse whisper. "Philippa," she said. "It was a top-level mission. I'll get in such trouble if anyone finds out that you know."

"What would they do?"

"I don't know—but I've heard some horror stories lately."

"Like what?"

"Like about butterflies having their wings cut off!"

"Really? That's awful! Why would anyone do that?"

"I don't know," she said. "It's probably just rumors. But a fairy can't live without its wings."

"What happens?"

Daisy shrugged. "I don't know. Some say you're left to wither and die. Others say you get turned into a human, but at the same age that you are as a fairy—which is pretty scary if you think that a lot of fairies have been around for over a hundred years. Not easy suddenly having to learn to live as an old woman of a hundred and seventy-five with no money, no home, and no way of getting by."

I shuddered.

"Exactly. Not something you want to get first-hand knowledge of." Daisy got up and lifted the window. "Listen, I really need to go," she said. Then she stopped. "Hold on," she said, crossing the room to my bed. She reached into her pocket, then lifted the pillow. It looked like she was putting something under it.

"What are you doing?" I asked.

Daisy put the pillow back in place. "Sorry. I thought I'd dropped something." She went back to the window. "I'll see you tomorrow, OK?"

"OK," I said. "Be careful."

She picked up the feathered charm and, holding it carefully, bent down and crawled out through the window. Stepping out onto the window ledge, she turned back to smile. "Watch this!" she said, holding on to the drainpipe.

I sat on the floor and waited to see what was going to happen. A moment later, Daisy let go of the drainpipe and held her arms straight out. Within seconds, an explosion of color snaked around the edge of her body, making a shimmering star shape with Daisy in the middle. The colors sizzled and spat and sparkled into a haze of blue and pink and purple — changing constantly, flashing and bursting all around her.

Then, as suddenly as it had started — it was over. The lights stopped. Daisy had vanished. In her place, fluttering for a moment outside the window, stopping just long enough to dip a wing as though waving good-bye, was a butterfly. The very same one that had come to our house. It really had been Daisy. She'd flown all the way to my house and managed to trick us into coming here on our vacation. I didn't even mind that she'd done it because of an assignment. I knew she'd done it because she wanted to as well. Because she wanted to see me as much as I wanted to see her.

I laughed with pleasure, smiling to myself. She was definitely the best, most amazing friend anyone could ever have!

I watched her disappear into the night, the feathered charm trailing behind her — almost twice her size, blowing gently on the breeze as she flew farther and farther away. The moonlight caught the charm, its colors sparkling in the night sky, tiny flickers of light flashing and glinting.

And then I realized something. The smile drained from my face. No! It couldn't be! I must be wrong!

I leaned out the window, peering into the night, straining to see clearly.

I watched carefully, holding my breath. Yes. I was sure. The material on the charm and Daisy's butterfly wings!

They were exactly the same.

ATC

"Can you see her?"

"I'm just checking now. Yes, I've got her here on my radar. She's on her way back."

"Has she got it?"

"It looks like it. There's a very strong indication of something coming with her, and it's showing a perfect match for us. I don't know what it is, but my SuperCell says it's one hundred percent linked with this mission."

"And she's bringing it back?"

"Yes, she's coming through the village now. She's heading for the river, coming past the shops. Hold on, she's stopped. Wait—what's happening?"

"What? What is it?"

"No, it's OK. I think she's just stopped for a rest. She's moving again."

"Good. We need her here as soon as possible."

"Hold on. Something's not right. She's moving again— but in the opposite direction. And there's a voice. Can't pick up the words, but my SuperCell is showing strong recognition—and a warning light!"

"What is it? What's happening?"

"She—she's gone off the radar."

"What do you mean, gone off the radar? How can that happen?"

"I don't know. Perhaps it's just stopped working. Let's not panic just yet."

"She might be in trouble."

"We'll give it a few moments. I'm sure she'll be fine."

"And if she's not?"

"If she's not? We—we have no contingency plan."

"No contingency? With a top-level mission like this?"

"I know, I know. It looked like a straightforward maneuver."

"So what happens if it fails? If she's gone missing for good?"

"Look, calm down. We'll cross that rainbow when we get to it. We don't need to panic just yet."

"You'd better hope you're right—for everyone's sake."

chapter eight
THE ROOM IN THE BACK

Daisy!" I called out into the night. "Wait!"

She flew on, farther and farther away. "Daisy, wait! Come back!" I shouted, leaning as far out of the window as I could. But she hadn't heard me. She flew on and on, a tiny bright light in the sky, smaller and smaller. First a dot, and then she was gone.

I slumped on the floor beside the window.

"Philippa?" Mom's face appeared at the bottom of the stairs. She climbed up a couple of steps and poked her head through the trapdoor. Glancing first at the bed, she looked around the room and saw me sitting on the floor. "Darling, are you all right?" She hoisted herself up into the bedroom and came to sit down beside me.

"I'm fine," I said, suddenly realizing I'd better think of a good reason to have been shouting in the middle of the night. "Sorry," I said. "I was having a bad dream and thought I'd get some fresh air. Did I wake you?"

"It's OK, darling," she said, putting an arm around me and stroking my hair. "Poor you. You haven't been sleeping well, have you? First you sleep half the day away and then you have another nightmare." She cuddled me closer. "I know!" she said. "I've got some lavender oil in our room. Shall I put some on your pillow? It might help soothe you."

I shook my head. The last thing I wanted right now was something that would supposedly help me sleep. The lucky charm was supposed to help me sleep, and look how that had worked out!

"I think I just need to go back to bed," I said, getting up.

Mom tucked me into bed and kissed my cheek. "I used to tuck you in like this every night when you were little," she said, smiling down at me. "You slept as soundly as a baby. Now, just shut your eyes and sleep like a baby tonight, OK?" She kissed my forehead.

"Thanks, Mom," I said. I turned over, and she went back down the ladder.

But sleep was the last thing on my mind. There were too many thoughts getting in the way. Why had Daisy taken the charm away? What was so special about it? And was it really made of the same thing as her wings? Had I imagined that? Had my sleepy, dreamy mind connected them by mistake? Maybe I thought I'd seen Daisy's wings in the sky, but really it had been the feathered charm all along. It was so dark at night, I couldn't be sure.

By the time my eyes finally flickered closed and my mind stopped whirring like an out-of-control machine, I'd managed to convince myself I'd made a mistake. It must have been the charm I'd seen in the sky, not Daisy's wings.

Before long, all the thoughts and questions melted away, and I sank into a dreamless sleep.

"We'll come back for her at three o'clock," Dad said to Mr. Fairweather. He turned to me. "Have a lovely day, sausage."

"You, too," I said, before Robyn dragged me inside

the shop. We went over to her corner and slouched down into the beanbags.

"So, what d'you want to do?" she asked.

I'd half wondered about asking Robyn to show me Annie's house, but it was pouring rain again today, so a walk in the woods wasn't a great idea.

Even though the house had spooked me when I came across it on my own, now that I knew it was her house, it didn't feel strange. Someone as friendly and lovely as Annie could never have anything scary going on in her home!

Except — what was it Robyn told me her dad had said? She wasn't what she seemed. What did he mean by that?

Either way, something about the house intrigued me. It seemed that everything and everyone I met here had a hundred question marks following behind them.

I wanted to talk about fairies with her, ask her what she'd seen, but I decided I'd wait for her to bring up the subject. And I wanted to talk about the house, ask her if her room was the one in the attic — but this felt too sensitive, too. I got the feeling she'd clam up on me again if I was too direct. I already knew her well enough to know she'd open up about things when she was ready to, not when she was pushed into it.

"You choose," I said.

Robyn jumped out of the beanbag and reached down to pull me out of mine. "Come on—let's hang out upstairs," she said. "I'll show you our apartment."

We were heading for the door that led out of the back of the shop when her dad called her over. "I have to duck into the post office," he said. "Promised Mrs. Metherson I'd get this book to her by tomorrow. Will you girls keep an eye on things for me for a few minutes?"

"Sure, Dad," Robyn said.

The doorbell tinkled behind him as he scuttled out with the package under his arm. Robyn took up her place on a high stool behind the counter. "How can I help you?" she asked in a funny voice.

I laughed. "I'm looking for a rare book," I said, playing along.

"Absolutely," Robyn trilled. "Rare books are our specialty. What is it you're looking for?"

I thought for a moment. What could it be? I wanted to think of something crazy and outlandish. But then I had another thought. Maybe I could find out more about something I really, actually wanted to know about.

"Butterflies!" I said. "I want to know all about butterflies."

As soon as I'd spoken, a shadow fell across Robyn's face. She stopped smiling, stopped playing along.

"What? What is it?" I asked. "What have I said?"

Robyn tried to wave it off. "No, nothing. Sorry," she said. She forced her mouth into a smile, but I wasn't convinced.

"Robyn, you can talk to me, remember? What is it? You can tell me anything."

She slumped on her chair, suddenly looking small and frail. "It's just — well, Mom used to love butterflies. We even had a butterfly house in a shed in the back."

I pictured the backyard. I couldn't remember having seen a shed.

"Dad tore it down after she died," Robyn said, reading my mind. "It was the same day he had the argument with Annie. It was so awful. He came home and went out into the garden. I'd never seen him in a mood like that. It was as though he had a black cloud over his head, following him around.

He got an ax from the back porch and went straight outside with it." Robyn looked up, her eyes faraway and sad. "He went over to the shed and smashed it to pieces," she said.

"What about the butterflies?"

She shook her head. "They'd already gone, anyway. When Mom got sick, Annie used to come over and look after her while Dad was at the shop. A few days before—before the end, Mom said she couldn't look after the butterflies anymore, so Annie took them away. She said she'd look after them."

That explained one of the things I'd seen at Annie's. All the butterflies flitting around the house.

"What happened then?" I asked.

"The shed collapsed after about three swings of his ax—but he kept going. I tried to make him stop. I was yelling and screaming at him, but it was as if he didn't even hear me or see me. It was as if I wasn't there. He just kept going. Smashing it into smithereens. When he'd finished, he was filthy and sweating. He stood looking at the smashed-up bits of wood all over the garden. Just stood there."

"What did you do?"

"I was scared. I'd never known my dad to do anything like that in his life. Eventually, he turned to me — but it was weird. It was as though he was looking through me, past me to something else. His eyes were a million miles away." Robyn shivered. "Then something changed. Like he came back to the present or something. He looked down at his hands, at the ax. Then he looked back at me. He said he was sorry. Then he took the ax inside and came back out with some trash bags and started cleaning up. He said, 'We'll burn this in the fireplace. It'll keep us warm,' and I just nodded and helped him clean it up. We burned it that night."

Robyn fell silent. I didn't know what to say. I wished I hadn't mentioned butterflies and brought it all up. I loved it that she could talk to me like this; it made me feel special and made me want to tell her all sorts of things about myself as well. She looked so sad, though, and I wished we could get back to how it had been earlier, having fun and laughing. But now that she was talking about the house, it made me think of something else, too.

"Can I ask you something?" I said.

"Of course," she said vaguely.

It didn't feel like the right time, but then there

probably wasn't a right time, and I really wanted to know. "Did you have the upstairs room?" I asked.

Robyn looked at me blankly.

"At your old house," I said, my face flushing with awkwardness. "Was your bedroom the one in the attic?"

"Yeah," she said. "Why?"

I smiled. "I thought so. That's where I'm staying."

Robyn smiled back. "Cool," she said. "I'm glad."

She hadn't lost that faraway look in her eyes, and I was still trying to work out how to lighten things up again when the doorbell tinkled and a woman came in.

"Hello, dear," she said to Robyn with a smile. "Are you running the shop today?"

"Only for a bit," Robyn said. "Can I help you?"

"I wondered if I could order a book. It's for my niece. She's living abroad and has asked me if I could get hold of it for her. Now, what was it called? Hang on — I've got it written down in here somewhere." While the woman rummaged in her bag, I wandered around the shop. There were so many books crammed onto every shelf, and piles of them were on the floor, too.

Robyn caught my eye. "Just a minute," she said.

"I'll just use the bathroom," I said. "Where is it?"

"Through there, second door on the right. Go through the stockroom, and it's at the back."

I turned to go.

"Wait. You'll need this." Robyn reached under the counter and brought out a set of keys. "It's the long one with the yellow tab."

I took the keys.

"Ah, found it!" The woman pulled a torn piece of paper out of her bag and handed it to Robyn as I let myself out through the back of the shop.

Second door on the right, through the stock-room. I fumbled for the key and pushed the door open. Wow! It was crammed virtually from floor to ceiling with books of every shape and size. Boxes and boxes were stacked on top of one another, no doubt containing more books. There were probably almost as many books in here as there were in the shop!

I took a step toward the back of the room, tripping over a single wide box in the middle of the floor. I pulled myself up — and that was when I saw it! Hanging from a hook on the wall, just inside the door.

No! It couldn't be. I must be mistaken!

I took another step toward it. I needed to see it more clearly. I stepped over a box on the floor and leaned across. It was! I was sure of it! A feathered charm just like the one in my room, the one Daisy had taken. In fact it was so similar, I could almost have sworn it was the exact same one — if that hadn't been impossible!

Surely it wasn't possible. I took another step toward the charm and leaned across a stack of boxes. It was just out of reach. I stretched across to grab it, then suddenly a shadow fell over the room.

I looked up, snatching the charm and grasping it in my hand behind my back.

Mr. Fairweather was in the doorway. His face was dark and full of shadows, and his small black eyes trained on me as he said in a voice like a knife cutting across my skin, "What do you think you're doing in here?"

chapter nine
THE DREAM CATCHER

I—I—I needed to use the bathroom," I stammered. I clutched the charm in my sweaty palm.

"What's that?" he asked, pointing behind me.

"What?" I tried to look behind me without turning my body.

"In. Your. Hand," he said, slowly and deliberately, as though he were talking to someone really stupid. Maybe he was. Maybe I was a complete idiot. I certainly couldn't make sense of anything that was going on right now.

"I—it's nothing," I said nervously. My voice quivered and shook. That's one way to make sure you sound guilty.

"Show me," he said. He held out a hand and took a step closer toward me.

"I just thought it looked nice," I said, my words tumbling out of me. If I could get the whole explanation out before he took it, maybe I could get out of this without being hurt. "I was on my way to the bathroom and had to climb over these boxes, and I just thought, ooh, that looks pretty, maybe I could take a closer look. That's all."

Mr. Fairweather was standing in front of me. His left eye twitched as he glared at me. "Give it to me."

I figured I'd run out of options. I gave him the charm.

Mr. Fairweather took it from me, smoothing it out in his palm. "You've squashed it," was all he said.

"Sorry — I didn't mean to. I —" I wanted to ask what it was doing here. Up until last night, it had been in my room. At least, I was pretty sure it had. Maybe I'd gotten it wrong, and this was a different one altogether. That would make much more sense. I hadn't really had a chance to look at it before he'd come in.

I gathered all the nerve I could and took a deep breath. I could feel the words clogging up my throat.

Come on, just ask. What's the worst thing that could happen? I didn't want to think about that.

"Where did you get it?" I asked.

"Where did I get it?" he repeated, his eyes lost and far away. Then he shook himself. "I bought it," he said. "I buy and sell. I run a secondhand shop, in case you hadn't noticed."

It didn't seem like the right time to point out that it was a secondhand *book*shop, and that this wasn't a book! I kept quiet.

"Now, hurry up and do whatever you came in here to do," he went on as he turned to walk away. Pausing in the doorway, he added, "And then I think you should leave."

"But I — I only just got here," I said.

"Robyn has to help me in the shop. We're busy this week. I shouldn't have said she could see you. You need to go," he repeated.

"But I wanted —" I stopped myself. *I wanted to talk to Robyn*, I was going to say. I was desperate to carry on our conversation from yesterday, find out what she knew about fairies, tell her what had happened to me. Tell her about Daisy — if it wasn't disloyal of me to do that.

I went to the bathroom and tried to figure out

what I was going to say—not just to Robyn but to my parents, too. I looked at myself in the mirror, feeling like a thief caught in the act, creeping around someone else's belongings.

But, hold on a second! What exactly had I done wrong? I'd picked something up that I was pretty sure had until last night been *mine*. Well, OK, not exactly mine—but it wasn't as if anyone else was coming to claim it. An abandoned old feathery charm stuck in the ivy on the side of the house. *I'd* found it. And now I'd seen it again—if it was the same one. I wasn't even doing anything. I was just looking at it!

Would Robyn see it that way? Would she still want to be my friend, or would my curiosity have ruined her trust in me? One thing was for sure: I wouldn't find out by standing in here!

I slunk back into the shop. Robyn came running over. "Dad told me about bumping into your parents at the post office," she said.

I glanced at her dad. He nodded quickly at me. Was he letting me off the hook so Robyn wouldn't see me as a sneak and a thief? Or was he trying to come between us by making me lie to her? Either way, I didn't have much choice. I wasn't about to contradict him and say that actually I'd been sent home because I'd been caught snooping in the back room!

"Yeah," I said. "Apparently they want me to go back."

"I know. That's too bad."

"Maybe we could meet tomorrow or something," I said lamely.

"Robyn's going to be busy tomorrow," her dad replied before she'd even opened her mouth. "Inventory time," he added.

"Well, I'll see you whenever," I said, aware that Mr. Fairweather was itching for me to get out of his shop.

"Come by tomorrow, anyway. I'll get him to let me off for a bit," Robyn said, quietly enough that her dad wouldn't hear. "Anyway, we've still got so much to talk about!" she added meaningfully.

"I know!" I said. *Fairies!*

Mr. Fairweather had come to the door to usher me out. "OK, bye, now," he said. "Thanks for coming over. Sorry you couldn't stay longer."

Hypocrite. Liar, I murmured under my breath. Then I pulled up my collar against the rain and ran back to the cottage.

*　　*　　*

I went to bed early that night, hoping Daisy would come soon. Why hadn't we arranged a time? I had no idea when to expect her. All I knew was that I needed to see her. She had to explain all of this before I really did go crazy!

Had it been my charm in there? The more I thought about it, the more I thought it couldn't have been. I mean, it didn't make sense. I'd found it at the house he used to own. If he'd wanted it that badly, he'd have taken it with him, wouldn't he?

Unless he forgot about it till they'd sold the house and it was too late. . . .

But even so — why would he want a weathered old charm like that? Whichever way I looked at it, I couldn't make any sense of it. And the more I thought about it, the more I could see it from his point of view — and it did look pretty bad, actually. Me snooping around in his stockroom. I decided I'd go over in the morning and apologize.

I looked at the clock. Eleven-thirty. Where was Daisy? I was getting so sleepy. I got out of bed and stuck my head out the window to get some fresh air and keep myself awake. *Daisy, where are you? I* whispered to the silent night sky. It didn't reply. The cloud cover had broken up slightly, and a couple of stars peeked down through the gaps. I stared at them, wondering if they were just normal stars or something to do with fairy godmothers. *Do you know what's going on?* I whispered to them. They didn't reply, either.

Past midnight. My eyes were struggling to stay open. *Come on, Daisy. You promised.*

It wasn't like Daisy to break her promises. At least not the Daisy I knew. Or thought I knew. Maybe I was wrong. I'd been wrong about me and Charlotte. I thought we'd be friends forever and ever, and all it took was a few months apart and we were like strangers now.

Perhaps the same thing would happen with Daisy. I thought about last night and tried to figure out if she had changed. There *had* been something different about her. She'd been edgy and nervous. Was it because of work? Or something to do with me and Robyn? Was she jealous? I hoped she knew she didn't need to be.

Please come back and see me, Daisy.

I couldn't stay awake. It was after one o'clock. Daisy obviously wasn't coming.

I snuggled down into my bed, pulling the blankets up to my chin, and nodded off into a light, jerky sleep.

"At last!"

Who was that?

"I've been waiting for you to go to sleep for hours!"

Daisy? Where was she? I tried to open my eyes.

"No! Don't! Keep them closed! Stay asleep!"

"Daisy?" I murmured.

"Yes. It's me. I've been desperate to see you."

"What do you mean, desperate?" I said. My voice came out in a thick, heavy drawl, as though it were being played on a CD with the speed slowed down. "Where have you been? I waited for you." The words crawled out of my mouth. I could see them! Inching away from me in a haze like a genie's puff of smoke, disappearing up, up, and away into the sky.

The sky? But I was in bed. Wasn't I? I looked down. I was standing in a glade in my pajamas. The sun shone down on the pair of us, lighting up a circle around us like a spotlight. But it was the middle of the night!

"Daisy, what's going on?" I said, feeling an itch of panic scratch at my skin. "Where were you? I waited for you. Waited as long as I could. But you didn't come."

"Listen," Daisy said. She took a step closer to me and looked into my eyes. "This won't be easy for you to understand, but I'm going to explain the best I can, OK?"

"OK," I said. Why was she talking to me as if I were a baby? And how was she going to explain any of this?

"Something really bad has happened," she said. "I was on my way back to ATC, and I stopped for a moment in the village. Carrying that thing wasn't easy. It was twice my size. It would be easier as a fairy. I was looking around to check that no one was nearby, so I could turn back into a fairy."

"Go on. What happened?"

"I got caught," she said.

"Caught? What do you mean?"

"Caught. Trapped."

"I don't understand! How did you get here if you got trapped?"

Daisy stared at me for a moment. Then she said in a calm voice, "I didn't get here."

"What do you mean?" I squealed. "You're standing right in front of me! Of course you're here!"

"I'm not," Daisy repeated, "And neither are you."

"Neither am I?" I said with a laugh that bordered on hysterical. "I'm not here? I think I'd know if I —"

"You're dreaming," Daisy said patiently. "You're asleep. This is a dream."

I looked down at my feet. Bare feet. I was in my pajamas in bare feet in the forest, standing in a glade with Daisy in the sun — in the middle of the night.

"I'm dreaming?" I said as it dawned on me that she was probably telling the truth. "But — but I don't understand. It feels so real. And you didn't come." I sat down on the grass. It felt soft and cushiony. As I settled into it, it turned into one of the beanbags from Robyn's shop. Daisy sat down next to me.

"I'm going to tell you everything," she said. "But I haven't got long. It's only a ten-minute dream, so you have to listen and concentrate, OK?"

"OK," I said, but I was already starting to feel sleepy again. The beanbag was so warm and comfortable and — ouch! What was that? The beanbag had turned into a hedgehog, spiking into my back. "Ow! Stop it!" I said. It became a beanbag again, and I settled back down.

"Daisy, how did you get here?" I said. "What's going on?"

"Do you remember last night when I was leaving, I said I thought I'd forgotten something?"

"By my bed?"

Daisy nodded. "It wasn't true. I was sprinkling some dust under the pillow."

I stared blankly at her. "Dust? You put dust under my pillow?"

"Dream dust," Daisy said. "Like I did the day before, too. I dropped some in your shoe to pass on a message so you'd leave your window open for me."

She put dream dust in my shoe? What was she talking about? I was about to ask her when I remembered. "The Scrabble letters!" I said. "You made that happen?"

Daisy nodded.

"But how? Daisy, I don't understand!"

Daisy took a breath. "You know yesterday, I told you I'm in Triple D?" she said.

"And you refused to tell me what that was."

"Yes. Well, I'll tell you now. I don't think I've got anything to lose in my present circumstances."

I wanted to ask what she meant by her present circumstances, but I didn't want to interrupt again. I needed to understand what was going on.

"It's Dream Delivery Department," she said. "That's what I do now. That's what butterflies are. They're fairies delivering dreams."

"All butterflies?" I asked.

"Most of them. In the summer, the retired ones come out, too. They're the ones everyone can see. The rest of the year, we're only visible to believers."

"Believers?"

"In fairies," Daisy explained. "Everyone else thinks butterflies are alive only in the summer."

I let out a breath as I tried to take in everything she was saying. "So you deliver dreams?" I said.

Daisy nodded.

"Gosh," I said. "So this really is a dream. This is a dream that you delivered to me?"

"Well, not exactly. Like I said, I snuck it under your pillow yesterday. I used some spare dream dust. I always carry a bit around, just in case."

"In case of what, though?" I asked. "What happened? Why didn't you come?"

"Listen, we haven't got much time, Philippa." Daisy's eyes held mine. "I'm in danger, and right now, you're the only person who can help me."

"I'll do whatever I can if you're in danger."

"OK, listen. I can't tell you everything, or I'll be in the kind of trouble I just can't get out of — but I'll tell you as much as I can."

"I'm listening," I said.

"Yesterday, after I left you, I was heading back to ATC with the dream catcher. I knew I had to —"

"What's the dream catcher?" I asked.

"You know the thing you had hanging in your room, that I took away?"

"Uh-huh," I said. "The charm."

"That's it. But it's not just a charm. I checked it against the MagiCell on my way up to ATC. I shouldn't have, really. My instructions were just to get it back. Not that I've managed to do that, either."

"So what did you find out?"

"Just that, really. That it's called a dream catcher. And that in some parts of the world, they use them to ward off evil spirits and bad dreams."

Ward off bad dreams? It hadn't exactly done that for me!

"In other places, they just sell them as toys or for decoration. But this one is different. This one is special."

"How do you know?"

"Because I was ordered to fetch it — by ATC."

"So what happened? Who caught you?"

Daisy hesitated. "Philippa, you're not going to like this," she said.

"I don't like any of it! I don't see why it would make any difference who —" And then I stopped. The shop, the stockroom, the dream catcher on the wall. "It's him, isn't it?" I said. "It's Robyn's dad."

Daisy nodded.

"But why? What's he got to do with it?"

"I don't know. I don't know what he wants, but whatever it is, it's not looking good for me."

I could feel anger start to swirl inside me. "Where are you? What did he do to you?" I asked, my chest tight and sore.

"He took me back to the shop. Earlier, when you came in — I was there! He took the dream catcher and put me in a jar. Philippa, I can't live long in here."

"How long can you survive?"

"I don't know. Maybe another twenty-four hours or so. Please, Philippa, you have to get me out of here!"

I felt the determination well up inside me, clogging up my throat. "Of course I will!" I said. "I'll do whatever it takes."

Daisy was starting to fade. Her face turned paler, the edges of her body were growing fuzzy and indistinct. "Daisy, what's happening?" I yelped. "Are you OK?"

"It's fine. It's just the dream — it's coming to an end. Listen carefully. I'm not in the stockroom anymore. That must have been a temporary measure. I think it's the only room downstairs that he can lock things away in. But he's moved me now. I'm in the apartment. He's got an office in the attic, where he keeps all his personal files and everything. I'm in there, in a cupboard or something. I think it's locked. It's hard to tell. It's dark — and there's not much air to breathe, either. Please, Philippa — hurry."

"How am I going to get to you?" I asked, panicked. What if she ran out of air before I got there? I couldn't lose Daisy — not again!

"I don't know. Find a way. Make him let you visit Robyn. Then you'll have to think up some way of sneaking up here."

"I'll do it," I said.

"Look, there's something else," she said in a whisper so faint I had to strain to hear her. Her voice was starting to fade as well now. "When he brought me up here, he took me out of the jar for a few moments."

"Why?"

Daisy paused for ages. I thought maybe I was losing her altogether. The dream had ended. But then she spoke again. "He was measuring my wings."

"What? Why would he do that?"

"I don't know. But he was muttering something about needing them more than I do. Philippa, I think he wants to cut them off. I think he wants to use them."

I remembered what I'd seen in the night — the way Daisy's wings had shimmered in exactly the same way as the dream catcher. And the dream catcher was torn. Did he want to replace it with Daisy's wings?

"But why?" I said again. It didn't make sense.

"I don't know," Daisy said. "I don't even want to think about it. All I know is I won't survive without them — if I ever get out of here alive, that is."

"Daisy — don't talk like that! I'm going to find you. You'll be OK. Do you hear me?"

Her face was fading even more. "I hear you. Just hurry."

I took a breath. "I'm going to find you," I said firmly. "After everything you've done for me — I owe you."

"You don't owe me anything," she said. "Just your friendship."

"You've got that," I said, a lump jabbing into the words as they formed in my throat. "You've got that always."

Daisy smiled feebly before fading even further. Moments later, she was gone. For a few seconds, I was standing in the glade all on my own. Then something *really weird happened. Everything went blurry and faded—the trees, the glade, all of it, faded and disappeared altogether.*

The next thing I knew, I was waking up in my bed. The window was open, and I could hear the wind outside, blowing through the trees with a soft whistle.

It was morning, and I had a job to do.

I was getting weaker. How much longer could I survive in here?

Philippa—please hurry.

I slipped and stumbled in the darkness. No use trying to get out of here. Any attempt to escape would only use up the tiny amount of energy I had. I had to stay still, try not to do anything. Try not to think about where I was, what was happening. Try not to make sense of it or ask questions. Right now, there were no answers.

Philippa, please—find me!

I could feel my body trembling. Dream dust sprinkled from my wings as they shook, falling softly around me onto the bottom of the jar.

Please . . . please, Philippa.

chapter ten

THE WOMAN IN THE PICTURE

I know you said you were busy doing inventory, but I wondered if there was any chance that maybe I could hang out with Robyn, just for a bit."

I was standing inside the doorway of the bookshop, talking to Mr. Fairweather in my best, most polite, I'm-very-sorry-and-I'm-actually-a-nice-girl-really voice. It wasn't that much different from my normal voice, because I *am* actually a nice girl, really. But when you're faced with someone really scary who shouts at his daughter in public places and has got your best friend trapped in a jar, it's not all that easy to act natural.

"I'm sorry about yesterday," I added nervously. "I didn't mean to snoop."

He looked at me from his seat behind the register, his eyes vague and distant, as though he were looking right through me at something a long way away. Then he turned back to the book he had open on the counter. Slotting a bookmark in between the pages, he closed the book. "She's upstairs," he said. "I'll call her. Wait here."

He went to the back of the shop and opened the door. Without taking his eye off me, he called up the stairs. "Robyn, your friend's here."

I heard a muffled voice call back down.

"You can go on up," he said.

"Thank you!" I scurried past him and ran up the stairs. That was one hurdle out of the way. Now all I had to do was sneak into his office without being noticed, find Daisy, free her from the jar, and get out again in one piece. Simple.

Robyn was at the top of the stairs, waiting for me. "I thought I might not see you again!" she said.

"Why would you think that?" I asked.

"Oh, I don't know. I thought my dad might have scared you off. Or . . ."

"Or what?"

Robyn looked down and fiddled with the hem of her sweater. "Or maybe you thought I was stupid, because of what I was saying the other day. About fairies and stuff."

"I didn't think that was stupid at all!" I said. "I wanted to hear more!"

"Really?" Robyn said as she led me along the narrow hall toward her room. As we walked, I noticed the staircase that led up to Mr. Fairweather's office. It was dark and narrow with just one door at the top. Closed. I prayed it wouldn't be locked. Somehow I had to find an excuse to get up there without Robyn—or her dad—knowing anything about it.

We went into Robyn's room. It was at the front of the apartment with a big sash window. Outside, the sky was white. Virtually bare trees poked over the tops of the shops on the other side of the square, their branches hanging limp and tired, as if drained of all their energy now that they'd lost their leaves, ready to spend the winter resting and waiting to come to life again. To the left, I could see the river that ran along the edge of the village.

"Come and sit down," Robyn said. Her bed had a pink quilt. The floor was littered with books, and a few clothes were strewn across the carpet. She picked them up and motioned for me to sit on the cushions under the window.

I snuggled into the cushions, and she sat on the edge of her bed. "Can I really tell you what I know?" she asked me. "You won't make fun of me?"

"Of course I won't make fun of you!" I said. "I believe it, too." I wanted to tell her about Daisy, to prove that she could trust me. But it felt too risky. Not now. Not while she was trapped upstairs in a jar, running out of air. I shuddered. No, I couldn't think about that now. I'd find her. I'd save her. She'd be OK. Everything would be fine; I'd make sure of it.

Robyn's eyes shone with excitement. "Well, it was a couple of years ago. I didn't know what it was at the time. I was in the woods with Mom. We used to go for walks together."

She stopped and swallowed. "Sorry," she said. "It's hard to — you know, especially at the moment. With it being so close to the anniversary, she's been on my mind even more than ever."

"It's OK," I said softly, wishing I could think of something more useful to say.

Robyn took a breath and nodded, as though

making a deal with herself. "Anyway. So I saw something in the woods. I thought it was a rare bird at first. I only saw it from a distance. I pointed at it and asked Mom what it was. She's really good at birds." Robyn caught herself. "She was, I mean," she added.

"Go on."

"Mom said she couldn't see anything. She said I must have imagined it. And then she said we should take a different route, because the way we were going had a lot of prickers up ahead. She took my hand and walked us off in another direction, talking to me nonstop all the way. It was like she wanted to distract me."

I couldn't help feeling disappointed. That was it? A rare bird that she'd seen in the distance?

"But I glanced back over my shoulder while she wasn't looking," Robyn went on quickly. "Then I saw that it wasn't a bird at all. Whatever it was, it came to land in a clearing. It was way bigger than a bird! It had wings, but they sparkled and crackled like fireworks as it landed! It was a fairy, Philippa. I know it was. I saw it with my own eyes!"

"What did your mom say?"

"I grabbed her arm and tried to get her to turn around, but she started running ahead. 'Race you to the oak tree,' she said. That was what we always did. It was our favorite tree in the forest. I tried to stop her, call her back, but it was as if she didn't want to know — or didn't want me to know. So I let it go."

"You didn't mention it again?"

Robyn shook her head. "I could tell the subject was off-limits. That's how it was with my mom sometimes. If she didn't want to talk about something, there was nothing you could do. She closed up like a book."

I thought Robyn was a bit similar in that way. I didn't say anything, though.

"We've got some books in the shop about fairies," Robyn said. "They've got lots of pictures. One of them had a picture that looked just like what I saw. That was when I knew for sure."

I suddenly had a thought. She'd given me an opportunity. "Why don't you get the books?" I said. "We could look at them together if you like."

"Really? You want to?"

"Sure," I said, hoping I was managing to disguise

the quiver in my voice. This would probably be the only chance I'd get, and I couldn't afford to mess it up.

Robyn jumped up off the bed. "OK, I'll get them now. Back in a sec."

"Get them all!" I said, hoping that would mean she'd have to spend some time rummaging around.

She smiled. "Do you want to help me look for them?"

"I don't know where they are," I said quickly. "Anyway, it's so nice snuggled up against your radiator! I'll wait here. Is that OK?"

"Of course," she said, heading for the stairs. "I'll see you in a minute."

The moment I heard her feet on the stairs, I was up. I waited till I heard the bookshop door close behind her, then I darted across the landing and up the dark staircase. *Please be open, please be open,* I muttered as I approached the door. It was an old-fashioned brass knob. I turned it. Nothing. *Don't be locked — please!*

I tried it the other way. Locked. No! I looked all around me for something that might help. There was a ledge running along the top of the door. Just out of reach. I stood on tiptoe and jumped up, grabbing at the shelf. There was something there — I could feel it.

I jumped up again, trying to grab whatever was there. Just missed it. One more try. I jumped up, swiping my hand across the shelf — and I got it! Something fell to the floor. I reached down and grabbed it. The key!

My hands shook as I slotted the key into the hole and turned it.

I pushed the door, and it opened easily. I was in! My heart was thumping so loud Robyn could probably hear it from downstairs.

Keep calm, keep calm. I took a deep breath.

The office was dark. A small window might have let in some light except that it was behind the huge desk, which was piled so high with books and papers they blocked half of it. I could hardly see. I didn't dare put the light on, though. I didn't want to draw any attention to myself.

There was a cupboard in the corner. That must be it. I crept over to it and carefully pulled at the door, wincing as it squeaked open. More papers, more books. Old folders that looked as though they hadn't been touched for years. But no jar.

Where was she?

I had to find her before Robyn came back. *Daisy, where are you?* I whispered to the silent room. I listened for a response of some sort. Anything! But there was nothing.

Searching around, my eyes fell on a shoe box on top of a pile of books. Could she be in there? I tore it open. More papers.

Where was she? Spinning around, I spotted a filing cabinet behind the door. How had I missed it? I pulled at the top drawer. It slid open. Rows and rows of folders. No jar. I grabbed at the second drawer. Nothing. Kneeling down, I slid open the bottom drawer — and there it was! The jar!

"Daisy!" I cried. I lifted the jar as carefully as I could. I was right. There she was inside, lying limp and lifeless at the bottom of the jar. *Please don't be dead. You can't be dead!*

I opened the jar — and the butterfly crawled along the bottom, slipping and limping. I turned the jar on its side. "Come on, Daisy. You need to get out!" I whispered.

She crawled along the side, edging her way to the top. As soon as she was out in the air, her wings fluttered gently. "Right. Let's get you out of here," I

said, holding out my palm so she could crawl onto my hand. But she didn't. She fluttered feebly and flew haltingly back into the drawer.

"Daisy, what are you doing? We've got to get out of here!" I said. I went to pick her up, but she hopped around on the bottom of the drawer. It was as though she were trying to tell me something. "What? What is it?" I asked urgently. I looked where she was hopping. The bottom of the drawer was covered in something—it looked kind of like the colored sand you could use in art projects.

"What is it?" I asked. "What are you trying to tell me?"

She stopped still in the middle of the sand, feebly batting her wings. It looked like the kind of sand Charlotte and I used to pour into a bottle to make a rainbow.

Rainbow sand? I looked again. Yes, it was multi-colored, like the rainbow of colors that explode around Daisy when she transforms into a fairy. Could it be . . .

"Is this the dream dust?" I asked. "Is that what you're telling me?"

Her wings slowly beat together. *Yes.*

"What about it? You want me to take it?"

Again, the wings came together, applauding me. I'd read her mind correctly. Despite everything, I was glad for that. It proved something to me. But I didn't have time to stand around congratulating myself. I had to get out of there — and I had to take some dream dust with me.

I glanced around for something to collect it with. There was a box of tissues on the desk. I stretched across and grabbed a handful. Carefully wiping the dream dust into a tissue, I folded it over, put it in my pocket, and reached over to the desk to put the box back.

I was about to turn back to the filing cabinet

to get Daisy and get the heck out of there when I noticed something on the desk that made me go so cold it felt as if my skin had turned inside out.

A picture frame. A photograph of a smiling woman. I grabbed the picture and stood holding it in my hand, frozen to the spot. No! It couldn't be!

I stared and stared at the picture. There must be a mistake. The photograph — it wasn't possible!

"What are you doing?" Robyn was in the doorway.

I didn't reply. I couldn't. I kept on staring at the photo.

She took a step into the room. "Philippa, what on earth are you doing in here? In my dad's private office?"

I tore my eyes away from the photograph to glance at her. She had a stack of books under her arm. The fairy books.

"Robyn, I —" What could I say? There was nothing at all I could say.

"What have you got in your hand?" she asked, taking a step toward me.

"Robyn — who is this?" I asked eventually, holding the picture out for her to see. "Who's this woman?"

"Who is she?" Robyn spat. "*This woman* happens to be my mom. How dare you come in here without permission and go through my dad's things!"

She snatched the photo from me.

"Your—?" I gasped, almost choking on the words. "Your mom? Are you *sure?*"

Robyn looked at me with utter scorn on her face. "Am I sure?" she asked. "*What?*"

"But—but it's—but she's—" I couldn't get the words out—but I had to. If I heard myself say them out loud, perhaps somehow I'd understand.

"She's what?"

"She—I've been having strange dreams since I got here. There was a woman in them—and it's her!"

Robyn looked at me as though she were looking at a piece of dirt.

"That's not funny, Philippa. Get out," she said calmly.

"Wait! Wait—listen to me. Hear me out," I said.

She folded her arms. "You've got five minutes. Then I want you to leave."

Five minutes. Right. I just had to gather my

thoughts — those that were at least vaguely within reach of adding up in my mind.

It was no use. I couldn't — they were too scattered. I was just going to have to tell her everything and hope for the best. I only had five minutes — and I'd used up the first one trying to figure out where to begin.

"I've been having strange dreams since I got here. I don't know why, and I don't understand what I was dreaming about. All I know is that I was trying to reach someone. There was a light, and a woman, and I had to get to her. Each time I had the dream, I woke up crying, feeling lost and lonely and so awful."

Robyn shifted uncomfortably as I spoke. Something seemed to flash across her face, but I couldn't tell what it was. Then her eyes hardened.

"Go on," she said, her voice brittle and sharp.

"It was the woman in the picture," I said. "I know it was her. Robyn, I dreamed about your mom."

I watched her face as I spoke. She seemed to be softening. I pushed on while I could see the doubt in her eyes. *Please forgive me, Daisy, but I need to tell. It's OK. Robyn believes. You can trust her. It'll be OK.*

"The other night, my best friend came to see me—"

"Your best friend?" Robyn interrupted. "I thought you didn't have one. I thought they'd both moved away."

"I know. I—look, bear with me for now, OK?"

Robyn sniffed and indicated for me to go on.

"She found something in my room, and she took it away, but before she could get back to ATC, she—"

"To what?" Robyn interrupted.

"It doesn't matter. The point is, she was captured by your dad. He—"

"What?" Robyn burst out laughing. "Captured by my dad? What do you think this is, *Chitty Chitty Bang Bang*?"

"Robyn, I'm going to tell you something now, and you have to believe me."

"I don't *have* to do anything!" Robyn snapped. She looked at her watch. "You've got one more minute. And I can tell you, so far you haven't said anything to convince me not to throw you out and never see you again."

"Look, she's a fairy, all right?" I spoke quickly. "She's a fairy. My best friend. She's a fairy god-mother. She gave me three wishes last time when she was a daisy, and now she's on a new assignment and she's a butterfly. And your dad trapped her in a jar."

For a moment, Robyn looked as though she believed me. Then she said, "So where is she now, your *fairy godmother*?" Her voice was heavy with sarcasm.

"She's in here!" I turned to the filing cabinet. "This is where he trapped her. I let her out of the jar. She's in the drawer. Look, I'll prove it."

All I had to do was show her Daisy. Robyn would have to believe me then! Especially after what she'd told me, about seeing all the flashing lights and crackling colors. That was exactly what happened when Daisy transformed into a fairy.

I knelt down and looked in the drawer. Where was she? I looked in the other drawer, on the desk behind me, all over the floor. Nothing. Nothing.

I looked at Robyn; she stared back at me with cold, disbelieving eyes. Holding the jar uselessly in my hand, I faced up to the awful truth.

Daisy wasn't there.

Y‌ou were saying?" Robyn's voice was full of needles. I hadn't heard her sound like that before. She could clearly switch into a furious mood as easily as her dad.

"She was here a minute ago," I said. "Honestly. You've got to believe me."

"Actually, I was about to, but I stopped myself just in time," she said. Her voice had changed. It sounded more sad than angry.

Please believe me, Robyn. Don't send me home without Daisy. I've got to find her. I've got to rescue her!

"What do you mean?" I asked.

"I mean you were about to make a complete fool out of me. But I'm not going to let you."

"No! It's not like that. I —"

"I trusted you," she said, cutting across me as if I weren't even there. "I told you things I've never said to anyone before. I told you I believed in fairies. I only said that because you said you believed, too."

"I *do* believe, too. That's what I'm trying to tell you, if you'll just —"

"And what do I get for my silly, stupid, childish trust in you? You just throw it right back at me, so you can make me look like an idiot."

"Robyn, please, I'm not trying to make you look like an idiot. It's true!"

"What? That your best friend is a fairy — oh, sorry, I mean a butterfly? And one minute you haven't seen her forever and the next she comes to visit you on your vacation? And she's here in this room, except — oops, no, she isn't, actually? What kind of person other than a complete and utter fool would believe something as far-fetched as that?"

When she put it like that, I had to admit it did sound a little crazy.

"I know how it sounds," I said. "But it's true. And she's in trouble. Your dad really did capture her."

"Oh, yes — my dad. How handy! Just because you saw him in a bad mood the other day, you think you can turn me against him? You don't know him! You don't know what he's really like. I told you that the other day. Don't try to make him out to be some kind of monster. And *don't* try to turn me against him!"

"I'm not trying to turn you against him," I pleaded. "He took her! He put her in this jar! Why else would it be here?"

"Search me," Robyn said. "Who's to say you didn't plant it there yourself while you were snooping around? In fact, while we're on the subject, he told me the real reason why you went home yesterday. He hadn't seen your parents at all, had he?"

I hung my head. What could I say? She wasn't going to believe me.

"He caught you snooping around, didn't he? I told him he must have been mistaken. I said you wouldn't do something like that. I managed to persuade him to let me see you again. I told him I knew I'd only met you a few days ago, but it felt like we'd known each other for ages. Felt like we really knew each other, understood each other, trusted each other." She threw her head back and laughed, her hair falling over her eyes. "How wrong and stupid could I be!"

"You're not wrong *or* stupid," I said limply. I was running out of answers. It seemed there was nothing I could say that would make her believe me. "Look, I can see it looks bad. But it isn't. Honestly. I am what I seem, what you thought I was. You can trust me, I promise."

She shook her head. "Sorry, but actually I can't. I can't trust you at all. Dad caught you snooping around yesterday, and I've just walked in on you doing exactly the same! I don't know what your game is, but it's 'game over' now."

"What do you mean? It's not a game!"

"Not anymore. I want you to go. And this time, don't waste your time coming back, OK? At all!"

She couldn't send me away now! I hadn't found Daisy! I had to convince her. "Look, please, Robyn. Don't send me away. Just help me look for Daisy. If we find her, I can prove everything."

"If we find her!" she snapped. "I tell you what — my dad was right about them all along."

"Right about what?"

"Butterflies. Vermin, he calls them. Ever since he smashed up that stupid butterfly house. I tried to tell him they're beautiful, magical creatures, but he wasn't having any of it. Well, neither am I anymore. I hope I do find your stupid butterfly. I'll stuff it back in that jar and throw it out myself."

What could I do? I was never going to get her to change her mind.

"I'll go and get my things," I said, and I headed back down the stairs.

"Yeah, you do that," Robyn said.

I went back to her bedroom to get my bag and shoved my hands in my pockets as I headed for the door. My fingers curled around the tissue in my pocket. That was when I had an idea.

Could it work? There was a slim chance — but what did I have to lose?

Robyn was on her way down the stairs. I had a matter of seconds.

I grabbed the delicate bundle from my pocket. *Please, Daisy, let this work,* I whispered to the dream dust. I quickly tipped half of it under Robyn's pillow, folded the rest into the tissue, and shoved it in my pocket. Then I turned to leave.

"Not gone yet?" Robyn was in the doorway.

"I'm going," I said.

She stood at the top of the stairs as I walked slowly back down toward the shop.

At the bottom of the stairs, I looked up. "Robyn, I —"

"Just go," she said. And with that, she turned and went back into her bedroom, closing the door behind her.

I lay on my bed, desperate to get to sleep. But the more I thought about how urgently I needed to be asleep, the more awake I was. And the more awake I was, the more I thought about all the things that had happened this week. Every day seemed to have gotten me further and further into this mess, and right now I couldn't see a way out of it. Apart from my plan. It was my last chance.

I checked under my pillow again. The rest of the dream dust was there. I just hoped it would work again.

Eventually, my racing mind wore me out, and I felt myself drift off into a turbulent sleep.

*   *   *

"You're here!" Daisy was waiting for me outside a huge white building. It had two enormous stone pillars at the front, and a real, live lion in front of each. They prowled around us as we talked, snarling and licking their lips.

"Don't worry about them," Daisy said. "They're not even supposed to be here. It's because the crystals were mixed up. They fell out of another dream. Sometimes if you mix dreams up, it can create really powerful images."

I tried to feel reassured. Still, I kept a close eye on them both, in case they came nearer.

"Was that what you were trying to tell me? To take the dream dust?"

Daisy smiled. "You read my mind," she said. "I just knew it might be my only chance to communicate with you."

"Why didn't you come out?" I asked. "Why did you hide?"

"Being in the jar had taken so much of my energy," she said. "Even if it wasn't daytime I don't think I could have transformed. Can you imagine how that would have looked? You find me, get all ready to prove to Robyn that I'm a fairy, and all I can do is hop feebly around on the floor. You heard what she said. I'd have been lying dead at the bottom of the trash by now."

"I guess so," I agreed. "How are you now?"

"Better. Not great. I tried to transform, and I still couldn't do it. I can hardly even fly. And I'm still stuck in this office. I can't get out."

"Why?"

"She must have told her dad what happened, and he came up and locked it. I hid in the closet when I heard him coming. I could see him from under the door. He wasn't very happy when he saw the jar was open and I was gone."

"What did he do?"

"Looked around everywhere, growling and snarling angrily. I hopped into a coat pocket, and luckily he didn't go through all his clothes."

"What does he want with you?" I asked.

"I don't know. I'm pretty sure it's got something to do with my wings. He wants them." Daisy shuddered. "I don't even want to think about it."

"Me, neither," I said, my heart heavy with despondency and dread. Then I remembered my idea! "Daisy — I put some of the dream dust under Robyn's pillow!"

Daisy stared at me. "What? Why did you do that?"

"I — I don't know. I thought maybe if I met up with you, you'd be able to go into a dream of hers and show her that you're real. Then she'd help us get you out of the office, and her horrible dad won't be able to cut off your wings. I know it's probably a stupid idea. I just —"

"Philippa, it's brilliant!" she said. "It's perfect! The only thing is — I can't go on my own. She'll just think it's a dream. You'll have to go first. I'll come in when you call me. Then she'll see that I'm a real fairy."

"You won't be too tired to transform?"

She shook her head. "We can do anything. It's a dream! We'll have to make sure it's convincing, though, so she knows you're telling the truth. Tell her everything. We'll show her I'm real. Then maybe you're right. Maybe she'll be able to stop her dad from cutting off my wings. Philippa, I'm not going to get out of here. I've got no strength left to do anything. As soon as he finds me, he'll cut off my wings and leave me for dead. I'm sure of it."

I swallowed hard. I couldn't think about what she'd said, or it would scare me so much I'd probably freak out and mess the whole thing up. We had one chance. "Daisy, I'll convince her. I will. I'll make sure of it."

"OK. I'm going to disappear for a bit and see if I can find out what kind of a dream she got tonight and if she's in it yet. As soon as she is, I can bring the two dreams together. Watch for her — you won't have long."

"OK," I said. "Good luck. You'll come back, won't you?"

"Of course I will," Daisy said. "Proving to Robyn that I'm real is my only chance to get out of here alive!"

"Right," I said. "Let's do it."

Daisy met my eyes for a moment. And then I blinked, and she was gone.

The building turned into an airplane and started flying away from me. Behind it lay miles and miles of wasteland. Animals prowled around. As I watched, a lone tree grew, zooming up into the sky. Its long, thin trunk reached all the way through the clouds, and then leaves popped out, bursting into flowers full of color. Birds flew around the tops of the tree, tiny as dots against the clouds.

Around the tree, the wasteland lay still, stark, and bare. Just flat plains. Nothing and no one here except me. What was I supposed to do? Just wait here for Robyn to show up, or should I go and look for her?

I wandered around the plains. The ground was hot, burning my feet. Behind a sand dune, there were some boots. I sat down to put them on. When I stood up again, Robyn was in front of me.

"Where am I?" she said.

I met her eyes. They looked startled and bright. "You're in a dream," I said. "And I'm in it, too."

"Just my luck," she said with a sniff.

"It's not luck. I made it happen. I needed to see you again."

"What for? I've got nothing to say to you — in real life or in a dream!" Robyn turned to walk away.

I grabbed her arm. "Wait!" I said, spinning her around. The wasteland growled, the ground popping in hot bubbles, like mini volcanoes exploding all around us. It's just a dream, just a dream, I reminded myself. Nothing to be scared of. Now, do what you're here to do — and do it right.

I took a breath. "Look, this is serious. My friend's in trouble, and I think you're the only person who can help."

"Your friend the fairy, that is?" she said sarcastically. "Or your friend the butterfly?"

"Both! She's the same person. If you don't believe me, she can prove it to you herself."

I looked around at the wasteland. Where was she?

As I watched, the wasteland turned into a meadow, full of flowers. Colors everywhere, dancing in a breeze. A million flowers nodding and bobbing, dandelion seeds blowing away. A butterfly flew between them, weaving its way toward us.

"Daisy!" I said, my breath falling out of me in relief.

She flew right in between us. Then slowly, her wings grew larger, her body became elongated, bursting and stretching. All around her, lights spun off in every direction, whizzing across the field, filling the meadow with even more color and light. Every spark became a new flower, until the meadow was bursting with life.

Daisy hovered between us, her wings like the softest silk, fluttering gently. She flew once around us before coming down to land. She stood next to me and reached a hand out to Robyn. "Hello, Robyn," she said. "I'm Daisy."

For a moment, Robyn didn't speak. She stood with her mouth open, staring at Daisy, then looking at me. "Seen something like that before?" Daisy asked.

Then Robyn pulled herself together. "It's a dream," she said. "You're not even here!" She turned to Daisy. "And neither are you. You're just figments of my imagination. I'm dreaming."

"You are dreaming," Daisy said. "But this is real. I am real. I created these dreams so we could prove this to you. I'm —" Suddenly, Daisy fell to the floor.

"Daisy, what is it?"

She was writhing around on the ground, kicking out, waving her arms. "No! No! Get off me!"

I fell to my knees. "What's happening, Daisy? What can I do?"

"He's got me!" she said. "I had to leave the closet to pick up the rest of the dust so I could bring it all together into one dream. He must have been watching me. Philippa, he's got me! Help!"

I turned to Robyn. She was staring down at Daisy. "Look!" I said. "I told you! She's in terrible trouble. You have to stop your dad. You're the only person he'll listen to. Please!"

"It's just a dream," Robyn said mechanically. She sounded as though she was talking more to herself than anyone else. "It's just a dream." She said it over and over, like a mantra, trying to make herself believe it.

Daisy stopped struggling and fell limp.

"Daisy, what's happened?"

She didn't reply. She just lay there. As I looked at her, her wings began to fade.

"No! Daisy!"

"Please, Philippa, help me," she said, her voice a shaky whisper.

"Just a dream, just a dream." Robyn stared down at Daisy, repeating the words over and over.

Any minute now, it was going to be too late. I grabbed

Robyn's arm. "Listen, I don't care if you don't believe all that stuff about the fairies or the dreams or anything, OK? But believe in one thing."

Robyn folded her arms and turned away. "What?"

"Believe in friendship. Believe that there's someone who is my friend, just like you are, who I can talk to about anything, just like we can."

For the first time, I noticed a flicker of something cross Robyn's face. What was it? Doubt? Trust? Hope? I pushed ahead while I had the chance. "Believe that I care about her enough to know that I have to do anything I can to get her out of danger."

Robyn let out a long breath. "And suppose I do that. Then what?"

"Then wake up. Get up and go up to your dad's study. If he's not in there, if there's no butterfly in the cupboard, then you can forget I ever asked anything of you. You can forget you met me, if you like."

"And if he's there?"

"Then get him to tell you what he's doing. Get him to stop. Please! That's all I'm asking."

I looked down at Daisy. She had faded almost completely now. The meadow was drying out, and the flowers had all wilted and died.

"Robyn, hurry!" I said.

The meadow was a barren wasteland again. Daisy was gone. Would we be too late?

"If you're lying . . ." Robyn said.

"I'm not. I promise!"

"OK." She turned away from me and started to walk away. A second later she was gone.

I was on my own in the meadow. But it wasn't a meadow anymore. It was rubble. Concrete. Buildings appeared in the far corner. Skyscrapers — they were springing up all over the field, coming toward me, closing in. And then I was inside one of them, going down an escalator. Down, down. Under the ground. It was pitch-black. The escalator threw me off at the bottom, and I bumped to the ground.

Picking myself up, I reached out — walls on either side. I was in a corridor, in the dark. Like the one in my first nightmare. Similar, but different. This one had tiny lights all along the walls. They were candles, night-lights, just enough so that I could see my way along the corridor.

I was under the earth, following the snaking corridor on its twisting path. Turning and turning, right, left, back on itself — until it straightened out. It was long, like a hospital corridor — clinical and bare.

And at the end of it — that light again. It was even stronger than the light I'd dreamed about before, and I was even more desperate to reach it. A thought shot into my head like an arrow from a bow: I had to get there. I absolutely had to.

The light burned more and more strongly.

Then one of the lions was there again. Prowling around me, circling me. Don't think about it. It's not here; it's not real; it's not even meant to be in this dream. I pulled myself up to my knees and looked the lion in the eye. It stared at me, its green eyes hard as bullets. I stared back even harder. You don't belong in this dream, I thought to myself as fiercely as I could. You can't hurt me.

And then, with a bloodcurdling howl, the lion sprang

forward, hurling itself through the air toward me. You're not real! I thought. You're not real.

The lion froze in midair. Literally froze. It turned to ice. Then it shattered into a million pieces and fell all around me.

I stumbled closer to the light. I was almost there. I was going to make it. Suddenly I was surrounded by trees. I was in the middle of a forest. The light shone through the trees, dodging and skipping in between them, growing dim and then strong again, opening and closing like a fan. Branches fell in front of me, snapping and tumbling with every step. I didn't care. I was close now; nothing could stop me.

Slipping and falling with almost every step, I stumbled on. And then — I'd made it. I'd reached the light. I was inside it, right in the center of the light.

I felt around for something. The light was blinding me. What was that? A door. A handle. I reached out with both hands and turned the handle. Pushing gently, I opened the door.

Falling through the door, I landed in a heap on the floor.

I rubbed my eyes and looked around, trying to take in my surroundings. It was a small room. I'd landed on a rug in front of a fire. The fire crackled and spat. Logs were arranged carefully in the grate, and flames curled around them as heat filled the room.

A squashy sofa piled high with cushions faced the fire. There was a rocking chair in a corner, with a shawl over it. In another corner, an open staircase led up to a second floor. A mantelpiece above the fire was filled with figurines. All animals. A bear, a rabbit, lots of butterflies.

A hefty-looking front door was shut and bolted. On the other side of the room, another door was shut, too. How had I gotten in here? I stood up and walked over to the front door. Where was I?

I heard the door behind me creak open. Someone was coming in! I spun around. A woman. It was too dark to see her face.

"Hello, Philippa," the woman said with a gentle smile. She closed the door behind her and came into the light. "Were you looking for me?"

chapter twelve

THE DREAM MAKER

Annie!" I said with a gasp. "But — how — what — where —"

Annie laughed softly. Sitting down on the sofa, she patted a cushion beside her. "Come and sit down," she said. "Tell me how I can help you."

I sat down. "I don't know how you can help," I said. "I don't know why I'm here, or how I got here. I —" I stopped. Her eyes were looking so intently at me, they were almost burning into me. It felt as though she could see into the corners of my mind, into the parts I didn't even know about myself.

"Am I still dreaming?" I asked, feeling foolish.

Annie smiled again and nodded. "Philippa, you've gotten yourself into a very powerful dream here. Do you know that?"

"I — I think so," I said nervously. "Daisy said the dreams got jumbled up, and that can make them quite strong."

Saying Daisy's name jolted me. It was as though I woke up — although a part of my brain knew I was still asleep.

"Daisy!" I said, leaping off the sofa. "We've got to help her! I've got to get out of here. Please — you have to let me go!" I ran to the door.

"Wait a minute. Slow down," Annie said calmly. How could she be calm when Daisy was in trouble? "Come and sit down and tell me all about it."

"I haven't got time to sit down! We've got to help Daisy!"

"Daisy?"

"My friend. She — she's a —" I stopped. How could I tell Annie that my friend was a butterfly? It was bad enough having to deal with Robyn's reaction when I'd tried to tell her. Grown-ups certainly didn't believe in things like that! And then there was what Robyn's dad had said about Annie — how she wasn't what she seemed. I hovered in the doorway, my hand on the handle.

"Philippa, your friend . . ." Annie repeated.

I quickly weighed my options. What did I have to lose? I could trust her, or I could run the risk of losing Daisy—forever!

"She's a butterfly," I said, my voice thin and wavering like a tiny leaf fluttering in a breeze. "She's at Robyn's house. Her dad—he's—he's—"

Annie sat forward, her eyes full of concern. She wasn't laughing at me. She wasn't telling me that I was being silly. "He's what, Philippa?"

"He's going to cut off her wings," I said. Then I shut my eyes and chomped down hard on my lip. It sounded ridiculous—I knew it did—and I didn't want to watch her burst out laughing.

A moment later, I felt Annie grab my hand. I opened my eyes.

"Listen carefully to me," she said. "Do exactly as I say."

I nodded.

"I'm going to get you a drink. Drink it all immediately. It will make you wake up."

"What's in it? Are you going to poison me?"

"Philippa, you're in a dream. I can't harm you. But I can help you to come out of it. You're too deeply in the

216

dream to come out of it on your own. If you don't have
the drink, you'll be asleep for hours."

"We haven't got hours!" I moaned.

"I know," she said seriously. "That's why we have
to hurry. Now, have the drink. You'll wake in your bed.
Get up immediately and go to the bookshop."

Annie was already fixing me the drink. She passed it
to me. Purple liquid fizzed and danced inside the glass. I
looked at it nervously.

"Drink it," she said. "You'll be fine."

Could I trust her? Could I? *Then again, did I have any choice?*

"Hurry," she said.

I swallowed the drink in three big gulps. Almost immediately, the room grew fuzzy.

"Annie, what about you?" I said. "What are you going to do?"

"I'll meet you there," she replied, her voice coming from the other side of a wall springing up between us. "Just get to the shop, Philippa. We have to stop him."

A moment later, the room had disappeared, and I was in my bed in the cottage.

I sat up, panting, my heart racing as though I'd been running for miles. Staring at the walls of my room, I tried to gather my thoughts. Bit by bit, they came to me. Daisy in trouble; trying to convince Robyn — had it worked? Then Robyn going, Daisy fading, the lions, Annie's house.

Annie — what did she have to do with all this? What did she know? Remembering her words, I flung on some clothes. It didn't matter if I didn't have any answers yet. All that mattered was that I got to the shop in time to rescue Daisy.

* * *

As I crept past my parents' bedroom, I had a pang of guilt. They'd be so disappointed if they knew I was sneaking out on my own in the middle of the night. Not angry. I wouldn't get punished or anything. I never did. It would be one of those kitchen-table talks where we'd all discuss what I'd done and why I'd done it and see if we could brainstorm for some ideas about how I might have approached the situation more positively. And maybe a role-play where we'd act out a better way of behaving.

I knew I shouldn't be sneaking around in a strange village in the middle of the night. But I also knew that my best friend's life might depend on it — and that was a hundred times more important right now.

I tiptoed down the creaky stairs and opened the front door. Closing it softly behind me, I pulled my coat on, glanced around, and ran through the silent streets to the bookshop.

Now what? The front door was locked — not that I expected anything different. I scanned the windows. All locked. There was a small passageway beside the shop. I hurried to the back and tried the windows there. Locked, too.

Running back to the front of the shop, I banged on the door with my fists.

Nothing. The street stood just as silent as before. It was as though I were the only person awake in the whole world. Where was Annie? Was she coming? Had I really communicated with her, or had it just been a normal dream?

I banged on the door again. Then I bent down and opened the mail slot. *"Robyn!"* I yelled. My voice echoed into the dark shop. *"Robyn!"* I banged again, not caring who I woke up. I'd explain. I'd think of something. I'd have to. All I knew was that Daisy was in terrible danger, and I had to save her — if I wasn't already too late.

I curled up my fists and was about to bash on the door again when I heard something. I lifted the mail slot and peeked inside. It was Robyn!

"Robyn!" I yelled through the slot.

She opened the door. "You'd better come in," she said, letting me inside.

"What's happened?" I asked, panicked. "Am I too late?"

"I don't know," she said.

"What d'you mean?"

"He won't let me in. He's locked himself in the office."

"Have you tried to talk to him?" I asked.

Robyn nodded. "He just keeps sending me away and saying it's for my own good." She glanced shyly at me. "I told him what you said to me. At least what I think you said." She paused before adding nervously, "In the dream."

"I did," I replied. "I know it sounds crazy, but it was really me!"

Robyn pulled her hair behind her ears. Her face was pale, and her eyes were scrunched up and tired. "He just keeps saying it's not how you said. I don't know what's going on. I don't understand, and I don't know who's telling the truth."

"And Daisy?" I held my breath, waiting for her reply. *Please, please don't say I'm too late.*

"I don't know," she said. "He won't tell me."

I headed over to the door at the back of the shop. "Robyn, we have to make him understand what he's doing."

"I know, but —"

"But nothing. We have to stop him! She's my best friend!" I threw the door open and ran up the

221

stairs, three at a time, all the way to his office at the top of the house.

I tried the door. Locked.

"Go away, Robyn," Mr. Fairweather said from the other side of the door. "I've told you."

"It's not Robyn," I said, forcing my voice to sound braver than I felt. "It's Philippa. And I'm not going anywhere till you tell me what you've done with Daisy."

"Daisy?" he replied, his voice muffled and flat, as though he were beyond caring. *Way* beyond caring. "I don't know anyone named Daisy."

"The butterfly," I said. Then I swallowed and summoned up all the nerve I could find. "She's my friend. And you're harming her. If you don't stop, she'll die."

He didn't reply.

Robyn came up to the door to stand beside me. Leaning against it, she spoke softly. "Dad, you've always said you wouldn't hurt a fly," she said. "But if Philippa's telling the truth—"

"I *am* telling the truth!" I interrupted.

"If it's true," Robyn went on, "then you're harming more then a fly. You're harming a . . ." She looked at me.

"A fairy!" I said. If Robyn couldn't speak the truth out loud, I certainly could.

"I don't understand," Robyn said, so quietly I wondered if he'd hear her at all. "Why would you do such a horrible thing? I would never have thought you could be so cruel."

We stood by the door, waiting in the dark for a reply.

Somewhere downstairs, a clock ticked. There was no other sound.

And then, a shuffling noise on the other side of the door. A key turning. Mr. Fairweather opened the door.

He looked at Robyn with eyes so dark and heavy they seemed to weigh his whole face down. "Cruel?" he said. "You think I'm cruel?"

"What else am I supposed to think?" Robyn asked.

He shook his head. "I can't have you think that. I can't." He walked away, leaving us in the doorway. "Cruel? My daughter says I'm cruel," he muttered. "And there's nothing I can do about it." He had something in his hand: the photo of Robyn's mom.

He slumped into the chair, leaning on the desk

and resting his head in his hands. He looked like an old man.

I don't know what I'd expected. Maybe that he'd be screaming and shouting—he'd have Daisy in his hand, squeezing the life out of her, a razor in his hand, ready to chop off her wings if I said a word. I don't know. But certainly not this: a broken man, huddled over a picture of his dead wife in the dark.

"I can't. I can't have her think that," he said. He was talking to the photo! "Forgive me, my darling, if this is wrong. I can't live with the lie anymore."

Then he turned to us. "All right—I'll tell you why I did it," he said. "I'll tell you everything."

I folded my arms and waited.

"It was for you," he said, looking Robyn in the eyes. "All of it. I did it for you."

"We agreed from the start that we wouldn't tell you," he said, still looking at the picture. Who was he talking to? What was he talking about? Before either of us could ask, he went on. "Your mom had always said it would be hard for any child we had. But we wanted you so much. And then you came along and answered our prayers."

He turned to face us. His face was so long and drawn, it was as though the skin were falling off him. "We agreed we didn't want you to have the burden that she had. It was a wonderful gift, of course—but a burden, nevertheless. We asked them if there was any way we could stop you from having to take over when the time came. They said that luckily you'd inherited more of my genes, and it wouldn't pass to you anyway."

"Dad, what are you talking about?" Robyn said, her voice pinched and tight. "Who did you ask? Who's 'they'?"

He drew a slow breath, then looked down into his lap and let it out. Raising his head again, he looked her in the eyes. "ATC," he said.

"ATC? What's that?" Robyn asked.

I gulped. "ATC? Above the Clouds?"

Robyn's dad looked across at me, as if noticing me for the first time. "How do you know about ATC?" he asked.

"I—I just do," I said, summoning all the bravery I could find. "I don't have to explain to you. You're the one who needs to explain!"

He lifted his shoulders in a heavy shrug. "Anyway, we agreed not to tell you. You didn't need to know. No one's supposed to know. We did everything we could to protect you from it and let you have a normal childhood."

"Dad—protect me from what?" Robyn broke in. "What was the big secret that I didn't know?"

"About your mother," he said carefully.

Robyn stared blankly back at him. "What about her?" she asked.

He looked first at me, then at Robyn. In a low, calm voice, he said, "That she was the Dream Maker."

Robyn sat down on a box. I stood next to her. Her face had gone almost white. Her hands were clenched tightly together in her lap. "I don't understand," she said. "What's a dream maker? What are you talking about?"

"It's a job," Mr. Fairweather began. "A very important and special one. The Dream Maker creates the dreams that are delivered to everybody at nighttime."

"What? You're not making sense," Robyn burst out. "How can a job like that exist?"

Mr. Fairweather took a breath. "There's a different world out there, alongside ours," he said. "It's run from a place called ATC. Above the Clouds." He glanced at me. I stared back. I wasn't giving anything away — not till I had Daisy and I could set her free.

"It's run by fairies," he said. "Fairy godmothers, to be more precise. They have all sorts of different roles, and each of them is given assignments. Some are very short; some are much longer."

"Dad, what are you saying?" Robyn asked, almost choking on her own words. "That Mom was a fairy?"

He took off his glasses, wiped his forehead, then replaced them. His voice hoarse and shaky, he went on. "They come from nature. They can be different things."

"Like butterflies!" I interrupted before I could stop myself. We were running out of time, and I had to get her back! "Like my friend in the jar. Where is she? You have to give her back!"

He ignored me, and I knew he wouldn't give Daisy up till he was ready. The best thing I could do for her was to keep quiet till he'd told his story. I wished he'd hurry up about it, though!

"She was a tree," he said. "She was supposed to have a long, long life."

Robyn jumped up. "A tree? Mom was a tree? Dad, that's ridi—"

Then she stopped and clapped a hand over her mouth. She sat down again, almost falling back on to the box. "The oak tree," she said hoarsely.

"How did you know?" he asked.

"I don't know. I—of course. The oak tree," she repeated as she stared into space. "It's weird," she went on, shaking her head. "Now that I've realized it, it's as if I always knew. Always. I'm right, aren't I?"

Her dad simply nodded.

"But it—" Robyn stopped. Staring blankly ahead of her, she said, "It died." Her voice had taken on the same faraway tone as her dad's. "It became ill, just when Mom did."

"It died, and so did she," he said huskily.

The pair of them got quiet, both lost in their thoughts and their memories. I was desperate to get Daisy back. Where was she? How much time did we have? My eyes scoured the room, searching for her as Mr. Fairweather went on.

"Many years ago, something happened," he said. "One of the dream deliverers had an accident. It was your mother's fault, really. She hadn't been watching what she was doing. She was out in the yard, chopping some wood for kindling. One of the dream deliverers came into the yard, and your mother—well, it was the timing. She was swinging the ax and sliced one of its wings off."

"One of its wings?" Robyn asked. "You mean there were fairies out in my own backyard, and I didn't even know it?"

"They were butterflies," I said. "That's who delivers dreams." I turned to Mr. Fairweather. "Isn't it?"

He stared back for a moment or two before nodding. "Your mother was devastated. When a fairy loses its wings, that's the end of everything. It has no place in the fairy godmother world—or in any other world. But your mother wouldn't allow that to happen. She went straight to ATC and begged them to help."

"And what did they say?" Robyn asked, her eyes wide and focused on her dad.

"They gave the butterfly a special role. Changed her life cycle so that even though she could no longer deliver dreams, she could still help. They made her your mother's assistant," he said. "She did her job well. Your mom couldn't have managed without her, especially when she became ill. Around this time, ATC said she would take over the role of Dream Maker."

"Who would?" I asked. "The assistant?"

He nodded. "But back on the day of the accident, I'd discovered something. Later in the day, I was out in the backyard when I spotted something on the ground. It was the wing that had been cut off. Lying on the grass. I picked it up, and I noticed it had little particles of something in it. Well, at first I assumed it was just dust. But when I looked closer, I noticed it glittered and shone. That was when I realized what it was."

"Dream dust," I said.

"It stuck to the wing. I showed your mom, and we were both entranced by the beauty of it: a dream caught and held tight by a butterfly wing. I completely forgot about it after a while, but then—"

"But then, years later, you thought you would use that knowledge for your own ends." The voice came from behind me. I spun around.

"Annie!" Robyn cried. "What are you doing here? How did you get in?"

"You left the door open," she said simply. She was looking at Mr. Fairweather. "I knew you'd done something," she said. "All during this last year, I've wondered what it was. I knew Robyn hadn't had the dreams. Now I understand how you did it."

"Get out of my shop!" Mr. Fairweather growled, rising from his chair. "Get out of my house!"

"No, Martin," she said firmly. "I will not do as you tell me any longer. It has to end." Annie's eyes bored into him until he eventually sat back down.

"You stole butterflies. You cut their wings off and used them to hold the dreams back, didn't you?"

He didn't reply.

"You made a dream catcher from the butterflies' wings and used it to stop Robyn from having the dreams. Didn't you?"

Again, he refused to reply or even acknowledge her presence.

"And you got the idea from the day that your wife saved a fairy's life after it lost its wings."

"Annie — how do you know all this? How do you know about the butterfly?" Robyn cried.

Annie knelt down in front of Robyn. Reaching into her lap, she picked up her hands and held them in her own. She smiled gently. Then she turned around, loosened her shawl, and let it slip from her shoulder. All the way down her right-hand side, her back was lined with a long red scar, as though a part of her body had been torn away.

She put her shawl back in place. "How do I know about the butterfly?" she said, turning back around and glaring at Mr. Fairweather before meeting Robyn's eyes. "Because it was me."

Robyn got up and paced the room. She stomped across to one side and then back again, all the time shaking her head. "No, no, no," she said. "You're lying — all of you. It doesn't make sense!"

"I know — it's a terrible shock," Annie said. "It's going to take time to get used to it. But it's true. Tell her, Martin."

Mr. Fairweather looked at his daughter with such anguish it almost hurt to look at him. "That first night after your mother's death," he said, "you woke from a terrible nightmare, crying, howling. You sounded like an animal caught in a trap in the forest. Wailing, in such distress. Then the next night, it happened again. Worse, even. Of course, I knew you were grieving—but to go through such horrors at night as well as during the day—well, that just seemed cruel." He shot an angry look at Annie. "Too cruel."

"So what happened?" I asked.

"I went to Annie, begged her to let Robyn not have the dreams."

"You knew Annie had been made the Dream Maker?" Robyn asked.

He nodded. "Your mother and I never hid anything from each other. We knew ATC had decided to pass the job on to her. She'd been your mother's assistant for years. She was the obvious choice. I pleaded with Annie not to send you those terrible dreams, not to let them be delivered. Anything to spare you at least some of the pain you were in."

"And you wouldn't?" Robyn asked. "You made me have the dreams?"

"I sent them to you because they were the dreams you were meant to have at that time," Annie said carefully. "Without them, you would never have the chance to grow beyond them, to heal."

"And that's when you made the dream catcher," I said to Mr. Fairweather.

"It was a long shot. I had no idea whether it would work, but I remembered what had happened with the dream dust years earlier, and I gave it a go. I had nothing to lose," he said. "I hung it outside Robyn's window. Sealed the window frame up, just to be sure. And it worked! The dreams never came in. They were lodged forever in the dream catcher. I'd spared her at least that bit of sadness."

But Annie was shaking her head. "No, you didn't,

Martin. You spared her nothing! You stunted her. How many times has she cried since you made the dream catcher?"

He looked at Robyn. She'd stopped pacing. She was standing in a corner of the room. "I haven't cried once since then," she said mechanically.

"You see?" Annie said. "You think that means she's happy? You're a fool, Martin! The tears are there. They're inside her. If they never come out, she will never be able to leave them behind. What you did was far more dangerous than allowing her to have the nightmares she was due to have."

Of course! The nightmares! The last piece of the jigsaw fell into place. "I had them!" I said. "I had the nightmares!"

All three of them looked at me, each face a picture of confusion.

"On my first night, I tried to open the window," I said. "It was jammed. Because you'd sealed it so tight! I got it open in the end, but a piece of glass splintered off. It cut into something, and I brought it in."

"The dream catcher," Mr. Fairweather said.

"The glass had pierced it! Robyn's dreams must have leaked out through the rip! The ones you sent her a year ago." I turned to Robyn. "That's why I recognized your mom. That's why I woke up each morning feeling that my heart was broken," I said. "I had your dreams!"

"The dreams my dad tried to stop me from having," Robyn said.

Her dad went over to Robyn's side. "Because I love you so much," he said. Putting a protective arm around his daughter, he turned to Annie.

"After everything my wife did for you, this is how you show your gratitude."

Annie's voice was steel. "Martin, there's more than one way to show gratitude," she said. Looking at Robyn, she said more softly, "Robyn, my dear, you will come to realize that in time, I promise you."

The three of them were locked in some kind of battle — but I had other things on my mind, and I couldn't hold back any longer.

"Let her go," I said to Mr. Fairweather. "Let Daisy go."

He met my eyes. "It's nearly a year," he said. "I know what happens with anniversaries. The dreams are coming back. I've seen it. I've had them, too. Not as bad as last year, not yet. But they're coming. I can tell."

Mr. Fairweather stared vacantly ahead of him. "I hadn't thought of the anniversary when we moved. I thought the worst was over and you wouldn't get any more of those dreams. If I'd thought ahead, I'd have brought it with us. These last few nights when you started having bad dreams again, I began to wonder whether I could make a new one."

His eyes shone with an intense glare, his voice passionate. I hadn't seen him look this alive before. "And then what happens?" he asked. "The dream catcher comes back to me! Not only that, but with a butterfly alongside it to mend the rip and make it work again." He grabbed Robyn's hands. "It was fate, Robyn. Why else did I happen to be outside the shop just as she was there? I was *meant* to get the dream catcher back."

I tried to swallow — but my throat was so tight, it felt as if I had a boulder inside it. "She's my friend," I said limply. "You can't do it."

"I'm sorry," he said, hanging his head. "I know it's wrong. I *know* it is. I've always known it was wrong — I'm not an ogre, you know. Despite what you might think. It was all I could think of — the only way I could help my daughter."

"Martin, you're not helping her!" Annie snapped. "You're holding her back, don't you see? She has to go through it. It's like — it's like —" She looked wildly around the room, as though searching for something to make her point.

Her gaze reached the window, and she looked out. "That's it," she said. "It's like — if there's a river ahead of you, you can't get to the other side by pretending it's not there. You have to cross it. It's the only way! The only way out of this is to go through it—for both of you. You *have* to let Robyn have her dreams!"

"And you have to give me Daisy back," I added, the desperation hurting so much it was as if my insides were drying out and beginning to crack. "Please!" I held out my hand. "Please," I said again.

Robyn softly touched her dad's arm. "I understand why you did it," she said. "And in a way, I think it was sweet of you. But Dad, what about the butterflies?"

"The fairies," I corrected her.

"You've hurt them, Dad," she said. "Daisy's in a jar now. Dad, you have to let her go. It's not fair."

"But I have to fix the dream catcher—and I have a butterfly right here in the house! Just one wing would do it! I can't bear to let you have those dreams again. How could that be any more fair?" he cried.

"Annie's right, Dad. I have to go through it. We both do. And we've always got each other there to help."

Mr. Fairweather turned to face the window. Looking out at the night sky, he finally mumbled in a quiet, choked voice, "The closet."

Before he could say anything else, I'd flung the closet door open and started rifling through the clothes inside. Nothing. There was nothing there.

"Where? Where is it?" I screamed, panic setting my throat on fire. He didn't reply. "Help me," I said, pulling at coats and suits, hurling shoes out of my way.

A moment later, Robyn was beside me. "Philippa," she said, pulling a blanket off a box. I stared at the box for a split second, then grabbed it and pulled its lid off.

There it was — the jar.

Inside, Daisy lay motionless. Even after I'd taken the lid off, she didn't move. "It's too late!" I cried, collapsing on to the floor and shouting at Mr. Fairweather. "She's dead! You've killed her!"

Annie rushed over to my side. "Let me see." She held the jar on its side, gently tipping Daisy into her palm. "Come on, little one," she said softly. "You need to wake up now."

"Please, Daisy," I said, sobbing, "you can't die!"

"She's not dead," Annie said. "Look at her wings."

I looked at Daisy's limp, motionless wings. "What about them?" I asked. "They don't exactly look full of life."

"When a fairy dies, the wings lose all their color. Then they shrivel and start to turn to dust. Look: Daisy's still have their color. She's just stunned and tired. I'm going to take her back with me to rest. I've got the best resources." She turned to leave.

"Will you let us know what happens?" Robyn asked.

"She'll be fine, honestly. Why don't you girls both come over tomorrow?" She looked at Mr. Fairweather. "If that's OK with your father," she added.

He sat at his desk, shoulders hunched over. He didn't reply.

I stared at Daisy, lifeless and still in Annie's palm. "Please make her better," I said, my voice choked and raw.

Annie smiled. "I'll do my very, very best."

And with that she left, and all we could do was stand in the darkness and wait.

I was up and dressed before it was even light. What

time could I go to see Daisy? All I could think about was seeing her, and all I could do was pray she'd be all right.

I crept into Mom and Dad's room and knelt beside the bed on Mom's side. I knew she'd be slightly more likely to wake up.

"Mom," I whispered loudly.

She grunted and twitched.

"I'm going out to see Robyn," I said. Mom turned away from me. I stood up and leaned across her. "Is that OK?"

"Mmm," she said.

I decided to take that as a yes. Closing their door softly behind me, I ran downstairs, stopping only to leave them a note on the kitchen table. Something told me Mom wouldn't remember having a conversation with me. Then I ran around to the bookshop.

Robyn was looking out the window when I got there. She came straight out. I was relieved at that. I didn't want to face her dad this morning — or ever again, if I had the choice.

"Come on," she said, and we set off for the forest.

*   *   *

We walked most of the way there in silence — but it was one of the silences that felt OK. One where we were each wrapped up in our own thoughts, but where it was nice to have someone else nearby, thinking her own private thoughts at the same time.

The forest seemed quiet as we made our way to Annie's house — as though it were lost in its own thoughts, too. When we got there, Robyn led the way up the path. And it was strange, but the path didn't look scary today. I could still see the spiders' webs lining the way up to her door, but the sunlight was glinting on them, lighting up tiny droplets of dew, and there was nothing to be scared of.

As I looked at them, I could see how carefully they were woven around the cocoons and chrysalides. Maybe spiderwebs had something to do with dream making. Perhaps that was where dreams were stored before they were delivered. Whatever they were, I couldn't help marveling at the intricate, delicate structures — tiny miracles of construction. It was like Robyn had said: they were part of nature, and all of it was beautiful. I guess it just depended on how you looked at things.

Annie opened the door. "Come on in," she said. "She's just woken up."

She led us through the room that I'd already seen in my dream. But then she opened another door into a small bedroom, and I forgot about the room, the dream — everything else.

"Daisy!" I said, rushing over to perch on the edge of the bed. She looked even paler than usual, but she managed to smile.

"You came to see me!" she said happily.

"Of course I came to see you! Where else would I want to be on the second to last day of my vacation?"

"Some vacation, huh?" she said with a grimace as she tried to sit up.

"Now, now," Annie said, coming in behind me. "Today is pure rest. No sitting, standing, or flying allowed, right?"

Daisy nodded, and Annie went back out again, shutting the door behind her.

"Anyway, this trip worked out just fine for me," I said. "I got to see you again! And I made a new friend at the same time." I looked across at Robyn, and she shifted uncomfortably.

"I'm sorry I didn't believe Philippa at first," she said. "I thought she was making fun of me."

"Philippa wouldn't do that," Daisy said. There

was a slight sharpness to her voice. What was it? Protectiveness? Jealousy?

"No, I know that now. She's a good friend." Then she added, "You're lucky to have each other."

"We've *all* got each other now, haven't we?" I said, nudging Daisy.

She shrugged. "I guess so," she said reluctantly.

"I'm just really glad that Robyn has met you for real," I went on. "So she can see for herself how amazing you are, and what a great friend you are, and how special it is that you're a real, live fairy, and how she doesn't need to doubt her belief in fairies anymore!"

Daisy looked at me for a moment. Then she said, "Mm, well, I guess I am pretty special, when you put it like that."

"Exactly!" I said with a laugh. She tried to punch my arm but missed and started laughing, too. Robyn joined in as well, and soon we were all laughing together. It didn't matter if we didn't know what we were laughing at. It was the "together" bit that was important.

Without us saying anything, it was as though the ice had broken. Robyn sat down on the other side of the bed, and before long the three of us were swapping stories and secrets without taking a breath or caring about anything else. We talked about Daisy's assignments at Triple D, about all the other butterflies she'd met, about what I'd been up to since we'd last seen one another, about Robyn's mom and all the times that magical things had happened over the years without her realizing.

"It's funny — there were so many of them," she said. "At the time, there was always an explanation. Mom or Dad made sure of it. But now that I know the truth, it all fits together, and I can't believe I didn't know it all along!"

"There's so much I still don't understand," I said as Annie came back in.

"Like what?" she asked, sitting down in the rocking chair in the corner of the room.

"Like how you make dreams, for a start! And have those spiderwebs got something to do with it?"

Annie smiled. "I'm afraid that's not something I can share with you," she said. "All I can say is this: Nothing is wasted. Not a sight or a sound or an emotion or a thought. Somewhere along the way, every little thing can be transformed into a dream, with the know-how, the apparatus, and a dash of fairy-godmother magic!"

"Wow," I said, staring at her.

Annie laughed. "Anything else?"

"Yes, actually." There was one last thing that still troubled me.

"What's that?" she asked.

"How much did you have to do with the mission?" I asked.

Annie paused for what felt like ages. "I knew about you coming here," she said eventually.

"You knew? You knew that Daisy came to our house?"

Annie nodded. "She was sent as part of a mission that I'm involved with."

"But why did you want me to come here?" I asked.

Annie looked at me, then at Robyn. "You had to meet Robyn," she said. "She needed someone like you."

"Someone like me? What do you mean?"

Annie smiled. "I can't tell you more."

"So you arranged it all?"

Annie shook her head. "No, I was only a small part of it. I helped. I did everything I could to bring you together."

"You got us to come to the shop, didn't you?

The leaflets—they were specially for us?" Then I remembered something else. "That day at your shop, you phoned Robyn. That was so we'd meet?"

Annie nodded.

"But why?"

"I really can't tell you more. The assignment isn't yet over. You'll find out soon." Annie glanced at Robyn, then looked away again.

Daisy struggled to hitch herself up a tiny bit in her bed. "But if you were involved, how come you didn't know about the dream catcher?" she asked.

"Once the dreams have gone from me, I have no way of tracing them. That's how it is. That's simply how it works. I can't hold on to dreams. There's only one way you can do that—and that's the way your father found."

"With a butterfly's wing," Robyn said.

Annie nodded. "I always suspected something had happened, but I couldn't prove it. It was only after Philippa brought the dream catcher into her room and you visited her there that it came back onto ATC's radar."

"So my breaking the rules was a good thing?" Daisy said.

Annie laughed. "As is often the way," she said.

Then she stood up. "Come on, now," she said. "Enough. You two should leave. Daisy will be getting tired."

Robyn and I groaned in unison. "We only just got here!" I said.

"It's been well over two hours! Your parents will be wondering what's happened to you!"

"Can we come back later?" I asked.

"Tomorrow," Annie said. "Listen carefully. Meet me at the oak tree at noon. I'll come with Daisy, OK?"

"OK," I said. I leaned over to hug Daisy. Robyn shuffled forward, and they gave each other an awkward hug, too. "See you tomorrow," I said.

"The oak tree," Annie repeated. "Noon. Don't be late," she added. "There's one last thing we have to do before this assignment is over."

ATC

"This is it, then."

"This is it. We did it."

"Hold on. Let's not count our bubbles before they've burst."

"Near enough. One more day."

"The most important day."

"Absolutely."

"The day it's all been leading up to."

"True. It could still go wrong."

"You have tonight's delivery for the girl?"

"Ready and waiting to be collected."

"And there's nothing to stop it from getting there?"

"We've laid on a dragonfly team for protection."

"Good. Then everything's set. Let's all get some sleep. We've got a very important assignment waiting for us tomorrow."

Robyn pulled her coat closer around her as she kicked through the leaves. "I dreamt about my mom last night," she said as we walked.

"Really? A bad dream or a good one?"

Robyn stopped walking. "It was horrible. All I wanted was to reach her. I could see her, but she was on the other side of a wall. It was so high, and I couldn't get over it. She kept telling me not to try, that I should stay where I was, but I wanted to get to her. I was desperate."

As she spoke, a tear slipped out of her eye. "Philippa, it was awful," she said, wiping the tear from her cheek.

We walked on. As we walked, an occasional plop of rain began to drop around us.

"When I woke up, I thought I would break," Robyn went on. "Physically, actually, break," she said. "I've never felt anything like it."

By now, tears were falling freely down her face. She ignored them and kept on walking. The rain was falling harder, too. I wrapped my coat more tightly around me, wishing I'd thought to bring an umbrella or a hat. It had been sunny when we got up this morning.

We turned onto a new path — and there it was, ahead of us: the oak tree. Its branches dead and spindly, empty of leaves, it still stood proud and defiant, taking its place in the forest like all the other trees.

"Philippa, I don't know if I can do it," Robyn said. She held on to my arm.

"Come on, I'll be with you, and Annie," I said. *And Daisy*, I added to myself. I still wasn't sure about Robyn and Daisy. They'd gotten along OK yesterday, but I knew there was still some suspicion and jealousy between them.

We walked slowly toward the tree. They weren't there yet. Robyn slumped onto the ground beside the tree, on wet twigs and muddy leaves. I sat down and joined her.

She pulled up her knees and hugged them. "I just miss her so much!" she said. "I can't —" The rest of her sentence caught and broke as she dropped her head onto her arms and wept openly. "I can't bear it!" she cried. "I can't bear it!"

I put an arm around her and held her as tightly as I could. We sat there in silence, while Robyn sobbed and sobbed and I held her, wishing there was something I could do to stop her from being sad, but remembering the story about the butterfly getting out of its chrysalis. *The struggle will make her strong,* I reminded myself. I couldn't try to take it away from her.

The rain was pouring down on us now, lashing against our faces, howling around us. The wind lifted leaves into cyclones, spun them around, hurling them in between the trees. Where had this come from?

I wiped my face, which was wet and cold from the bitter wind—and then I saw them. Two figures coming toward us. The taller one holding the other one's hand. The smaller of the two was limping a little, walking slowly, her bright blond hair whipping around her head as she walked.

"Daisy!" I yelled. Jumping up, I pulled Robyn with me. "Robyn, they're here! Look—Daisy's out of bed. She's here!"

Robyn looked up. Wiping her face, she stood up. She grabbed my hand. "I'm so glad, Philippa," she said with a weak smile. I knew it was all she could manage right now, and it meant a lot.

A moment later, Daisy and I had fallen into a huge hug. "Are you OK now?" I asked her as Annie went over and wrapped Robyn into her arms. "Are you better?"

"She's not a hundred percent yet, are you?" Annie said, looking over Robyn's head at Daisy. "Another day or two to recover, and then it's back to work!"

"Slave driver!" Daisy said with a smile.

"Back to Triple D?" I asked.

Annie shook her head. "Daisy's wing was slightly damaged in the tussle with Martin. It'll be absolutely fine in time, but we decided it was best to transfer her to a different department. ATC is coming today to discuss it further. She'll get the highest possible recommendation from me, though."

I smiled at Daisy. She grinned back. "Annie'll make sure I get something good," she said.

"So, what are we doing here?" I asked.

"You'll see," Annie replied. She reached down to wipe the tears from Robyn's cheeks, then pulled her close again as Robyn continued to sob. The four of us stood close together below the branches of the dead oak tree, huddled against the rain.

"It's going to get worse," Annie said after a while. She had to raise her voice so we could hear her over the rain. I didn't know if she meant the weather or Robyn's grief, but as if to highlight her words, the wind whipped up even more fiercely and thunder grumbled in the distance.

Annie sheltered Robyn in the crook of her arm as Robyn cried and cried.

The storm was coming closer and closer. "Will we be all right?" I asked as a flash of lightning tore across the sky. "Is it safe to be out here in this?" I still didn't understand why we were here at all.

Annie looked up at the sky. "Any minute now," she said mysteriously. "Just wait a few —"

A growl of thunder broke into the rest of her sentence. Instantly, behind it, a streak of lightning split the sky. And then another, and another. And then —

Just like a giant spear hurtling toward us from the sky, the lightning struck the tree. Right in its center.

"Look out!" Annie called. She pulled Robyn away from the tree. Daisy and I were right behind them. We ran together toward a nearby tree. Its semi-bare branches weren't much shelter, but it was better than nothing.

From a few yards away, we watched in total silence as the oak tree creaked and cracked and moaned. Then it fell, and split in two.

Branches that had been reaching up into the sky only moments earlier bent and fell backward, stretching outward and falling to the ground. It was as though the tree were opening up its hands, opening up its whole self.

And then the strangest thing happened. From inside the tree, colors and lights burst out. They spun and unfurled from the very being of the tree, whirling around like smoke rising from a fire. More and more—blue, pink, gold, orange, green, jade, and silver—every color you could think of, flowing out, flowing and pouring out of the tree like lava running free and wild.

"What's happening?" Robyn asked. Her voice shook—but not with fear or with sadness. With something else. It was laughter. She was laughing. Soon I realized I was, too. We fell together into the colors, lapping them up like they were a million dollar bills fluttering around us. We danced and reached out for the colors, trying to catch them, to touch them. "What is it? What's happening?" Robyn asked again.

Annie went over to the tree. Walking right into the center of the dancing lights and waving the colors out of the way, she reached into the tree and pulled something out. A tiny parcel.

"This is for you," she said to Robyn.

"What is it?" Robyn's eyes were wide and shining.

"It's full of dreams. The happiest dreams you could imagine. All of your life, your mother saved them."

"For me?" Robyn asked.

"Every last one. Your mother wanted you to have them so much."

"Why now?" I asked.

Annie turned to me. "Any dreams a Dream Maker creates can only exist undelivered for a year after her death. After today, it would be impossible for you to have them."

"Why did you wait, then?" Robyn asked.

Annie took one of Robyn's hands. "Gifts like this from the fairy-godmother world have laws attached to them. You can only receive such dreams of happiness if you have first opened your heart to the sorrow inside it. The sadness opens a space inside

260

you — and the dreams can only enter if that space is open, if your heart is ready to receive them."

Robyn swallowed hard.

"That was why I sent you those dreams," Annie went on. "So you would be ready to receive this gift."

"What would have happened to them if she hadn't been ready in time?" I asked.

"They would never have been delivered," Annie replied. "Instead, they would have been released as pure energy with nowhere to go. And that would have been extremely dangerous."

"Why?" Robyn and I asked in unison.

"Such energy cannot exist in the human world. Without an open heart to enter, dreams like these turn to fire. Released here and now, they would have torn through the forest. The destruction they could have caused is unthinkable."

I shuddered.

"But you don't need to worry about that now. The process has begun. You have opened your heart." Annie held the parcel out to Robyn. "Take them," she said. "They're yours."

Robyn took the parcel and held it in her hands as delicately as if it were an injured bird.

"Inside this parcel is the most powerful dream dust you will ever find," Annie said. "Each single speck of dust holds a dream created especially for you, to use whenever you need it. Every one chosen with care, and with love. Think of it as a savings account that your mother created for you — fairy style!"

The parcel was wrapped in the most delicate silk wrapper. A butterfly's wing!

"But how . . . ?" Robyn's voice trailed away as Annie turned around.

"Thanks to my accident, we discovered the power of a butterfly's wing," she said. "We found a way to keep them safe." Opening up her coat, she revealed her shoulder blade — not the one she'd shown us yesterday, the other one. She had a matching scar running all the way down it — where her wing should have been.

There's more than one way to show gratitude, Annie had said. Now I understood what she'd meant. She'd cut off her one remaining wing so that Robyn's mom could ensure Robyn would have this amazing gift!

"What use is a butterfly with one wing?" she said simply.

"I don't know what to say," Robyn gulped. The tears on her cheek were drying now. The rain had slowed down, too.

"Just keep the parcel somewhere safe," Annie said.

"I'm going to make a necklace out of it," Robyn said. "Then I can have my mom close to me all the time. It will always remind me of her, and of you and the sacrifice you made for me." She rushed into Annie's arms, holding tightly on to her while Daisy and I stood and watched.

"Wait a minute." Annie pulled away from Robyn. She was looking beyond her at something. We turned to see what she was looking at. There was someone in the distance coming toward us. Robyn's dad! His face looked fierce as he strode toward us.

"Robyn!" he called. "Annie!"

No! After everything we'd been through — he couldn't drag Robyn away again. Not now!

Mr. Fairweather caught up with us and stood in front of Annie. Now what? Would they have a full-scale argument out here in the woods? Would he drag Robyn off again and forbid her from ever seeing any of us?

"Martin, please let's not do this," Annie said. "We said everything that needed to be said yesterday."

Mr. Fairweather looked at Robyn, then back at Annie, then at the rest of us. "No, we didn't," he said.

"Dad, please." Robyn reached out for her dad's hand, but he pulled it away.

"I need to say this now," he said. "Don't stop me, or I may never manage it again."

Then he looked Annie in the eye. He just stood there in silence for what felt like ages. Then in a voice so quiet we wouldn't have heard it if a twig had snapped at the same time, he said, "I'm sorry."

"Martin, I —"

He held up a hand to stop her. "I was wrong. I was terribly, terribly wrong. I did so many bad things in the last year. I can hardly remember what I've done. It's as though it was someone else. Someone else who came in and took over while I was lost. I'm sorry. I'm so sorry."

And then he started to cry. Silently at first, his shoulders hunched and shaking. Tears snaked down his cheeks. Soon he was moaning and holding himself as though in the most terrible distress you could imagine.

"Dad." Robyn ran into his arms, and this time he didn't stop her. He held her close, as though she was all that could keep him upright, as though he would fall beyond reach if he let her go.

Eventually, he loosened his grip and wiped the back of his palm across his eyes. He looked back at Annie. "I treated you badly. I'm truly sorry. Will you forgive me?"

Annie reached out and softly touched his arm. "Martin, I can forgive you easily enough. But the important thing is that you forgive yourself — and learn to live again. You know she would have wanted you to."

He nodded, and the lump in his neck bobbed up and down.

We stood in silence a few moments longer. The colors continued to spill from the tree, dancing in and out of the forest, flowing gently in long, rhythmic sweeps, gradually slowing down, coming to rest in a circle around the five of us.

Finally, the colors began to fade away, seeping into the grass. Raindrops tinkled from branches as the sun poked out from behind a cloud. A faint glow of sunlight opened up, peering shyly through the trees.

"Look!" Robyn pointed above us. A perfect arc was emerging. A rainbow, arching over the whole forest, as though holding us all together, keeping us safe.

Annie turned to Daisy. "It's FGRainbow2359 — the assignment is over."

"What does that mean?" I asked, knowing in the back of my mind what she was about to say — and praying I was wrong.

"It's Daisy's new supervisor," Annie said. "It means she has to go."

"But I don't want her to!" I said. I sounded like a baby — but I didn't care. Why did she have to leave?

Daisy swallowed. "I don't want to go, either," she said sadly. She came over to me, and I hugged her tight.

"She'll be fine," Annie said. "Really. I'll make sure of it."

"She really has to go?" I asked.

Annie nodded. "I'm sorry," she said, holding out a hand for Daisy.

Daisy gave me one more squeeze, then she went over to Robyn. "Look after Philippa, won't you?" she said. "Don't forget about her. I know she'll be going home again soon, but don't desert her like Charlotte did, or forget about her. She's really special."

Robyn nodded. "I know she is," she said. Then she smiled at Daisy. "And so are you. I can understand why she'd want you as her best friend."

Daisy blushed. "Well, I guess I've learned that having best friends isn't just about keeping them to yourself," she said. "It's about learning to share."

Robyn reached out to give Daisy a hug. "Thank you for everything," she said. "And don't worry," she added, smiling at me. "I'm not planning on deserting Philippa. We'll make sure we keep in touch — I promise."

"Come on, now," Annie said. "It's time."

"Annie," I said, my throat clogged up and burning.

Annie turned. "What is it?"

"Will I ever see Daisy again?"

Annie smiled. "I can't give you any answers for certain," she said. "But I can tell you this: when someone saves a fairy's wings, the favor is never forgotten."

And with that, she and Daisy walked toward the rainbow. Robyn and her dad stood together, their arms tightly around each other. I stood beside them as we watched Annie and Daisy walk away from us.

The sun shone so brightly through the rainbow I had to shield my eyes. When I opened them again, Daisy had disappeared.

Robyn and her dad were on either side of me. "I can't bear it," I said as they held on to me. It felt as though all the sunshine had gone out of my life, as though it would never come back.

And then I remembered Robyn saying exactly the same thing, earlier — that she couldn't bear it. That was when I realized I *could* bear it. Of *course* I could. It was just a good-bye. It was just a step along a journey, not the end of it. It was a parting, not an ending.

"You'll find a way," Mr. Fairweather said. "You'll be OK."

"I guess," I said.

"Come on," he said. "Let's close the shop for the afternoon and get your parents. I'll take you all out for some coffee."

Robyn looked at her dad as though he'd suggested we go and climb Mount Everest.

"I have to start living again," he said. "Annie's right. Your mother would never have wanted me to hide away in the shop, half-dead myself. It's going to be different from now on."

Then we turned and started walking back to the village. Mr. Fairweather walked ahead, while Robyn and I walked arm in arm, dodging puddles all the way along the path.

We came to a huge puddle right ahead of us. It ran all the way across the path, like a river, running from one side to the next.

If there's a river ahead of you, you can't get to the other side by pretending it's not there. You have to cross it. It's the only way.

I looked at Robyn. She smiled back at me. And then, without a thought for how cold or wet our feet were getting, we linked arms and sploshed our way through the puddle, all the way to the other side.

"I think you'll see her again soon," Robyn said, her boots squelching with every step.

I turned to watch the last bit of the rainbow as it began to fade, saw the light and the colors and the sunshine and the forest — all of them for what they were. The magic and beauty of everything.

Smiling, drenched, and cold, I turned to my new friend. "Do you know what?" I said. "I think so, too."

And with that, I looked back up at the sky one more time. As I watched, the rainbow glowed a moment longer, then threw one last hint of light through a break in the clouds — and was gone.

Once again, I can't claim to have written this book all by myself. Many usual suspects and a few new ones have helped along the way. Special thanks to:

Nancy Green for the elder tree;
Karen McCarthy for the fairies in the woods;
Mom, Dad, Caroline, Lee, and Min for those all-important final tweaks;
And Mary Hoffman, for her generous support and tortoisey encouragement.

And with extra, extra special thanks to the following:
Linda Chapman, for being utterly in tune with me, the story, and the characters;
Judith Elliott, for being the most fantastic editor, for making me chop out the deadwood, and for helping me join the dots;
Catherine Clarke, for always being there with advice, support, ideas, encouragement, time, effort, and friendship;
And Laura Tonge, for talking about fairies all year, whether over dinner when I had to make notes on a serviette, at seven o'clock on a rainy morning when I'd run out of ideas, or about a hundred times in between.

*The fate of both the fairy world and the
human world lies with Philippa Fisher.*

*Philippa Fisher and
the Fairy's Promise*

Liz Kessler

Book three in
the Philippa
Fisher series!

"Are we almost there?" I asked for the twenty-fifth time.

Dad gave me the same response he'd given me twenty-four times already. "Almost!" he said, smiling at me in the rearview mirror and giving Mom a nudge in case she hadn't noticed his funny reply.

I sighed and got back to reading my book.

But then I noticed something outside the window. "Wait!" I sat up a bit straighter. "I recognize this road." I leaned forward and looked through the front windshield. "It's the woods!" I said. "We *are* almost there!"

An excerpt from *Philippa Fisher and the Fairy's Promise*

"I told you we were," Dad replied.

"To be fair, you also said we were almost there when we hadn't quite reached the end of our street," Mom added.

But we were this time. We were on the outskirts of Ravenleigh. I felt a jiggle of excitement go through me. We were nearly at Robyn's house!

Robyn and I sat in her room above the bookstore her dad owns and caught up on all our news.

I couldn't help comparing it with what had happened when I'd gone to visit Charlotte the first time after she'd moved away. We'd spent a week not knowing what to say to each other. With Robyn, you couldn't shut us up if you tried! I don't know how we still had so much to talk about — but we did, and I wasn't complaining.

I checked my watch. Nearly six o'clock. "I'd better get going," I said reluctantly. Mom had told me to be back for dinner. "See you in the morning?" I asked as I headed down the stairs.

"Definitely! I'll come over as soon as I'm up."

"Great."

I was about to turn to walk through the shop to go out when something moving across the floor caught my eye. A mouse! It ran across the shop floor and right over to my feet!

I screamed and ran back to the stairs. The mouse followed me. I stumbled halfway up the stairs and the mouse tried to follow, but the steps were too steep and it kept falling back onto the floor.

It stood at the bottom of the steps looking up at me with tiny green eyes.

"I've never seen a mouse with green eyes," Robyn said. She'd heard me scream and was looking down from the top of the stairs.

"Me neither," I replied, although at this moment, I didn't care what color its eyes were; I just wanted it to stop chasing me.

"It likes you," Robyn said with a laugh.

"Well, I don't like it!" I replied. "Make it go away!"

"Look, it's got something in its mouth," she said, bending down and reaching out toward it.

"Don't touch it!" I screamed. Just then, the mouse dropped whatever was in its mouth, looked up at me once again, and scampered away.

I cautiously made my way down the steps as Robyn was examining what the mouse had left behind. It was a torn, crumpled-up piece of paper covered in mouse spit.

An excerpt from *Philippa Fisher and the Fairy's Promise*

"Nice," I said.

Robyn laughed. She dropped the paper into the trash as we headed through the shop. "See you in the morning," she said at the door.

"Can't wait!" And with that, I waved to her and to her dad, who was busily chatting with a customer. And then I headed back to the house for an evening of moussaka and Monopoly with my parents.

The next morning, Robyn was at the door before Mom and Dad had even woken up. Which isn't that amazing, really. When Mom and Dad are on vacation, you don't really get much more than snores and grunts out of them before lunchtime.

"Come on, let's go out," Robyn said. I scrawled a quick note, propped it up on the kitchen table, and followed Robyn outside.

We wandered around the village, talking and looking in shop windows. We paused outside Potluck, the pottery shop owned by Robyn's friend Annie. She used to be Robyn's mom's best friend, but Robyn's mom had died just over a year ago, and Annie and Robyn's dad hadn't seen eye to eye since then. They'd made up last time we were here, though.

An excerpt from *Philippa Fisher and the Fairy's Promise*

"How are things?" I asked nervously.

"Fine," Robyn said with a smile. "She and Dad are totally cool now. She comes over for dinner every Friday, and I'm allowed to see her whenever I want. She and Dad even go out walking together on the weekends sometimes."

"I'm so glad," I said. The shop was closed, but we stood looking at all the plates and bowls and animals in the window.

I was admiring a particularly handsome dragon when someone suddenly barged into me out of nowhere, knocking me forward so hard, I almost bumped into the window.

"Hey!" I spun around and came face-to-face with a woman staring into my eyes in a way that really creeped me out. She was hunched over, with an enormous multicolored shawl looped over her shoulders and over the top of her head, a tiny little face that you could hardly see because the shawl was spread halfway across it, and a pair of beady bright green eyes boring straight into mine.

Find out how Philippa and Daisy met!

Philippa Fisher's Fairy Godsister
Liz Kessler

"Sparkles with magic and charm." — *Girls' Life*

"The author of the Emily Windsnap books
offers another upbeat fantasy." — *Booklist*